For the amazing family, friends, and students who never stopped believing in me, and without whom, this dream would have never become a reality. To you all I cheer "Huzzah!"

THE STAND AT SARATOGA

REBELS, RENEGADES, AND RED COATS

A NOVEL BY
M.R. BONICK

WAR HAD BEGUN. It had been over two years since the first shots rang out on Lexington Green near Boston. It would be called by some "The shot heard around the world." Why? Was it so loud that peasants in France and the serfs in Russia could hear it? No, but they were definitely interested in the result. This war was different.

For one side this was a revolutionary war. These were the men, women, and children of America who were fighting for their freedom. They wanted to be independent from a king and country they felt no longer understood their needs. They wanted freedom from a government who continually passed laws that hindered their growth and trampled their attempts at equality. They wanted freedom from taxes that hurt their prosperity. They wanted the opportunity to participate in government, a right they thought they deserved, simply by being colonies of England. They wanted to be free of the constraints of social status. In America, a man could get rich by his deeds, not just because his father was rich or his father before him.

They shouted "no taxation without representation," "liberty or death," and "don't tread on me." They called themselves patriots. They came from every walk of life and many different countries. Their army consisted of merchants, farmers, tradesman, and even a few professional soldiers. Some had knowledge of combat, many of them didn't. Still they joined this war with the hope of gaining independence. They joined this war not knowing it would be monumental, not just for them, but for other countries as well.

For the other side this was a civil war, a war of rebellion. How dare the colonies turn their backs on their ancestors? How could they betray a government that was only trying to give them protection? Didn't they understand their responsibility to help pay for their own protection? These were England's colonies, and they would remain England's colonies. What would these settlers do without the king and Parliament to pass the laws for them? Did they really think they could run a country on their own? What kind of lawlessness would befall this land without the help of Mother England? Who did these "Yankees" think they were? They needed to learn a lesson.

They needed to be shown the futility in opposing the greatest army in the world, because their army *was* great. War hardened, well trained, and experienced. They were professionals, and they were very used to winning. Many of them fought this war because it was their job, and that is what they were ordered to do. Some who played a part on this side were called "loyalists." They fought because they felt it was their duty to punish the traitors for turning against their English homeland. Many of these people prospered under England's rule and didn't want change. To rebel against the king was to rebel against God. For them victory seemed to be just a battle away.

As is the case with any conflict, there were some on both sides that used this conflict to try and further their own desires. They were the most dangerous of all. The stakes were high, and the world was watching.

FORWARD

James Felton wiped the sweat from his brow as he gazed at the rapidly disappearing sun. His drenched hunter's shirt clung to him, giving evidence of the day's hard labor. "Why should today be any different," he mumbled. No matter how hard he worked he wouldn't trade it for anything. James gazed around at the green acres of rolling lush farmland that he and his family owned. *Land! My land!* James took a deep breath, sucking in as much of the clean air as he could. He exhilarated in the fresh scent of being out in the open. He could smell the water from the cool mountain streams that wound around the surrounding hillside. He would never get tired of the fragrance of an environment that was hardly touched. It reminded him how much better off his family was now.

The Feltons immigrated from England a few years earlier and eventually found themselves a home several miles northwest of a small town named Crown Point. Lake Champlain lay just a few miles to the east, its waters helping to make the area perfect for farming and transportation. James gazed to the west where the sun was diving behind the mountain peaks. The mountains ran in a snake-like line, as far as the eye could see, to the north and south.

For centuries land had been hard to come by in England and the rest of Europe. If a person's ancestors didn't own land, *he didn't* own land. It was an aristocratic system that trapped its prey into a life predetermined by those who came before. James Felton had bigger plans for himself. So he and his family, like thousands of others, leaped at the chance to move to America and make a new life. Gone were the days of working for someone else. He and his kin could now work for themselves. James had been an excellent farmer in England, so he took full advantage of the rich soil that was now his. He again wiped his brow and continued to slash furiously at the long strands of wheat with his recently sharpened scythe.

Soon his wife and children would be calling for him to come to dinner. The smell of tonight's feast was already reaching his nostrils, making his mouth water with anticipation. He wanted to get a little more done first. This year's crops would not only feed his family, but also fetch him a nice profit at the market. It would be a very pleasant winter.

James smiled as he thought about his family, which was growing at an alarming rate. He had left England with his wife, Margaret, and two young children. He was now the proud father of three more energetic boys with yet another child on the way. The children were able to help with some of the smaller chores, and soon they would be capable of handling *much* more. The Felton's would turn tidy profits with their abundant crops for generations. Soon people would be working for him. The land was perfect. The fact that this bonanza of green land had been lying across the ocean all of these years was astonishing. His ancestors had been toiling on ground not nearly as fertile, which made his accomplishment of being here even more satisfying. Of course, James knew that others had lived here before him.

When the Feltons had first arrived on the banks of Lake Champlain, they were informed the land they were to settle had once belonged to the Iroquois Indians who had since moved on. At first James was uneasy about having his family live on land that had been the property of the Iroquois Nation. The stories that had reached England about their ferocity were enough to give any man second thoughts. He had to be reassured by the local magistrate that the Iroquois had migrated to the west. James decided the risk was worth it. After a few years of making a decent home for his family, he hardly thought of them anymore.

He, like many of the others in the area, wanted nothing to do with the rebellion that had begun against the King George III and England. Oh, he certainly agreed that taxation without representation was unfair, but it was a small price to pay for the chance to own land. He was glad that most of the war was being fought further to the south. His area had seen some action when the rebellion started, but it had been quiet for some time now. There were rumors that a large British force might try to make their way down Lake Champlain, but James figured that it was more town gossip than fact. He wanted no part of it and why should he?

He was just about to head back to the house when an unnatural calm settled over the wheat field he was tending. He stood still and listened for anything out of the ordinary. He heard nothing, absolutely nothing. The chest-high wheat swayed with a gentle breeze that made it impossible to tell if something was actually moving within its tall stalks. *It is probably just a small animal trying to steal some food.* James gripped his scythe a little tighter in case he was wrong. It wouldn't be a very effective weapon, but it was all he had. His rifle lay against a weeping willow several yards away. He thought he saw something moving within the wheat stalks to the right of the tree. He couldn't tell for sure. The entire field remained still, like it was holding its breath for something.

James began to wade carefully through the wheat with his scythe poised to strike. He wanted to reach his rifle. He would feel safer then. Peering over the strands of wheat he moved warily towards the willow and his weapon. He crept to within ten yards of the tree when a flock of tree swallows burst from its branches arcing high into the darkening sky. The flight of the little birds startled James enough to make him stagger backwards and trip over a rock hidden underneath. He dislodged the rock and tossed it angrily towards the tree. "Fool birds!"

He stood and brushed off dirt from his tan breeches. He hoped his boys hadn't seen him act this way. Before James could take another step closer to the willow, he stopped in his tracks. An Indian! The brave was bare-chested with deerskin leggings and moccasins. The single line of hair running down the middle of his scalp identified him. Two long white feathers stuck up from the back of his head. He was a Mohawk, one of the clans of the Iroquois. *What is he doing here?* James didn't want to panic. The brave could be there for a number of reasons. *Maybe he wants to trade?* Some Iroquois would wander into town looking to trade, but this was highly unusual. *What does he want?* James wondered nervously. The brave made no attempt to move in any direction. He continued to stand in front of James blocking his path to the willow. The Indian was not holding a weapon, which prompted James to drop his scythe. If the Mohawk was friendly, James wouldn't help things by holding a blade, any kind of blade. Even after James dropped the tool to the ground, the Mohawk remained motionless. James held up his hand as a sign of friendship. There was still no reaction from the brave standing in his way.

A blood-chilling scream broke the silence. It came from the direction of the Felton house. *Margaret!* More shrieks cut through him like knives. *The Children!* The Mohawk let out a howl that blended with the desperate wails of his family. It was magnified by the rising crescendo of war cries that answered him, a terrifying sound that hammered at James's ears from all directions. He realized now that this encounter with the Mohawk *was not* friendly. He threw himself to the ground, snatching the scythe he had only a few moments before discarded. When he stood up to face the brave he saw that the Mohawk now held a nasty looking tomahawk. More frantic cries came from the direction of his house. *I have to get away! I have to go to them!* James reared back with the scythe to take a slash at the Mohawk. He never delivered the blow.

Just as his arm was about to descend it was stopped and held fast from behind. His hand was pressed into dropping the make shift weapon. James was whirled around from behind and brought face-to-face with the most terrifying Indian he had ever seen. The Mohawk who held him was twice the size of the other. He too had a shaved scalp except for a single line of hair that ran from the front to the back. Horrified, James observed a hideous looking scar that striped the man along the length of his bare chest. James tried to wrestle away from the Mohawk's grip, but it was useless. The enormous warrior looked down into his eyes and smiled. The panicked screams of James's family continued. He hit the brave with his free hand as hard as he could. The monstrous Mohawk didn't even flinch. The screaming stopped.

"I am called Anachout," the warrior growled. "In your tongue it means the Wasp. Time for you and the rest of the land stealing whites to feel my sting!"

"No! Please no!" James cried in anguish.

James Felton's dreams of owning land had cost him, and his family, their lives. The Mohawk warrior continued to stare into his eyes, while his free hand plunged a razor- sharp blade into the settler's stomach.

1

"The man is a mule," muttered Thomas.

"He isn't the only one," answered Ben.

Thomas picked up a rock and hurled it at his younger friend. "Who asked you?" Thomas Bowman had just finished the latest argument with his father over the legitimacy of the patriot cause. Elden Bowman had been very clear that he and his son were not going to become involved in the revolution that was sweeping across the colonies. Thomas couldn't understand how a man that fought for what he owned could just sit idly by and take whatever injustices King George and Parliament dished out. Even though they lived on a farm away from any major city, the taxes and laws that were passed in England still affected their livelihood. Thomas wondered why King George had to be so stubborn! All the colonists wanted were the same rights that every other Englishman had. How could it be wrong to give them representation in Parliament? Thomas agreed with his father that fighting should have been avoided, but as soon as it started, like all young men, he wanted to do his part.

When Ethan Allen and Benedict Arnold captured Fort Ticonderoga, Thomas celebrated the accomplishment. Afterward, the Continental Congress commissioned Robert Balderdash to lead a force north to try and take Canada from the British Army. Thomas, then sixteen, wanted very badly to go along with them, but was held at home not necessarily by his father, but by duty. The Bowman's had been struck by tragedy a few years before the war started. Thomas's mother and sister had caught smallpox, and after a long and vicious struggle they passed away. The Bowman men were left to care for each other.

"I'm just saying, Thomas, arguing isn't worth you getting upset. Your father *isn't* going to agree to fight."

"No, he won't. I have a better chance of getting King George to come over for tea."

"You could leave him and go on your own...like my brothers," said Ben sadly.

Thomas shook his head. "I can't leave him. He needs me. And your brothers may still turn up. Don't lose hope."

"I know, every day I expect to look out the window and see them walking towards the house. Your father needs *you*? Are you sure it's not a little of both?"

Thomas shrugged, but inside he knew Ben was right. After his mother and sister died, it didn't seem proper for him to leave his father alone, and he really wasn't sure he was ready to go off on his own. This was why, although old enough, Thomas didn't go north to fight with Balderdash like Ben's brothers had. The only way he was getting into this fight was if his father came with him.

As he looked back on it, it was best that he *did not* go with General Balderdash. The expedition had been a disaster, and many of his friends that went north did not come back, including Ben's brothers. It was because of this horrible mismanagement by Balderdash that the Continental Army was having a hard time finding anyone else in the area to join the war. Most would rather fight their own way then be lead by a man who seemed to have no clue what he was doing. To make matters worse, Balderdash thought a lot more of himself then anybody else, and he had a habit of only listening to those who had money and power. This did not go over well with the proud and tough people living around Lake Champlain and the Hudson River.

Thomas knew that going to war would not be easy, but now at age seventeen he felt a little guilty staying at home where it was safe, when others his age were fighting to help win freedoms he would also enjoy. These arguments with his father had gained intensity after New Hampshire was the first colony to declare its independence. It was shortly followed by the Virginian Thomas Jefferson's Declaration of Independence, which the delegates at the Continental Congress signed a year ago. While most everyone else in the area celebrated this accomplishment, Thomas's dad nearly had a heart attack. "Is there not an ounce of common sense in the entire bloody town of Philadelphia?" he had said. "The only bloody thing those fools declared was that they were ready to be hung! I'd like to see any one of them pick up a musket and go WIN that independence! Those hypocrites talk about freedom while half of them own slaves!" That was one day Thomas didn't even bother to argue back. When his father lost his temper it was best to find other things to do.

Still, even though Thomas knew it was useless, he continued to debate with his father about them getting involved. Their arguments had a way of making Thomas so aggravated that he was sure steam escaped from his ears. Rather than lashing out further against his father, Thomas calmed down by grabbing his rifle and heading to the woods to hunt. Sometimes Ben joined him. Ben was the youngest of the Sterling children. At twelve he wasn't old enough to go to war like the rest of the men in his family.

With a sigh Thomas looked at the rifle he had cradled in his arms. This was his most prized possession. The rifle had been given to him as a birthday gift a few years ago. His father purchased it from German gunsmiths in Philadelphia. It had a flintlock like the Brown Bess musket a British Regular carried, but there were a few significant differences. The barrel of the rifle was longer than a musket, giving it more accuracy. The barrel also contained ridges called "rifling" that held a musket ball tighter and made it spin as it was shot out of the barrel. The spin helped to create more speed making the musket ball move in a straighter line over a longer distance. These German rifles were well-balanced and much lighter than their English counterparts.

Another difference was the rifle had a compartment in the stock that kept the greased patch used in loading and firing. Both rifles and muskets fired lead musket balls, but a soldier using a musket loaded his weapon using a cartridge that contained both the firing patch and the ball. A rifleman kept the ball and patch separate. This also was a boost to greater range and accuracy.

As soon as Elden gave Thomas the rifle he began training him how to shoot it effectively. Thomas, left handed like his father, was a quick learner. His dad was very well-known for being an excellent rifleman, and more than once Thomas had heard others say that his dad was the best shot in this part of the colonies. Thomas promised himself that one day he would be better. He didn't have very far to go. At festivals, Thomas always won the younger division in target shooting, and could probably hold up very well against the older men, too.

At the moment, it wasn't a bull's-eye he wanted, it was a big buck. One that he could drag back to his father to maintain some dignity after his most recent failed dispute. They were naturally competitive with each other, even more so it seemed now that they were alone and constantly at odds over the Revolution. Thomas knew his dad was just trying to protect what was left of their family, but Thomas sometimes felt that he was too cautious, and treated him too much like a little boy.

Indeed Thomas was not a little boy anymore. He had grown considerably in the past couple of years. He was tall for his age, a trait that came from both of his parents who were more than average height. Life on the farm had shaped and toned his muscles, but there was also a hint that he would build more with age. His blue eyes and long red hair, tied in the back of his head, was a match of his father's. Thomas thought about how many times people commented that the two of them looked alike.

Elden and Thomas lived on a farm a couple of miles southwest from the town of Crown Point, which was at the southern end of Lake Champlain. The area was not as settled as many of the colonies further to the south, but with all of the waterways and the River Road along the Hudson, it was very easy to get to Albany if they needed things a small town could not provide. The woods and hills surrounding the area provided food, lumber, and peace and quiet when Thomas needed it. The area was once home to the Mohawk Iroquois, but they had long since moved on farther to the west. Once in a while they came into Crown Point for trade, but lately they had been keeping away.

    Crown Point and the surrounding area had seen quite a bit of excitement over the last few years. Lake Champlain and the Hudson River provided a link between Canada, the northern colonies, and the middle colonies. With forts being used up and down the waterways, this was a strategic spot for either army to hold. The most important of forts was Ticonderoga, which lay a few miles to the south. It guarded Lake George and access to the Hudson River. Once held, Ticonderoga was reputed to be impregnable. That was what made Ethan Allen's feat of capturing it so significant and embarrassing to the British.

Thomas figured sooner or later they would be coming to take it back. He had heard rumors that a British general named Burgoyne was planning to do so, but his father and others shrugged it off as town gossip. "They are more worried about important towns like Philadelphia and New York," his father had told him.

His father's insistence on neutrality was going to make him a spectator until things were over. Most of the area supported the patriot cause. There were some families that were loyalists, but most of them left as soon as the fighting started. There were others, like his father, who wanted to stay neutral and avoid trouble at all costs. Many of the men in the area including his father had fought alongside the red coats in the conflict with the French and their Huron allies. It was odd that now most considered the British soldiers the enemy.

Here in the woods it all seemed very far away. Thomas felt contentment when he looked around at the splendor that surrounded him. Healthy pines that reached high into the sky grew in abundance and filled his nostrils with their freshness. There were plenty of red oaks that produced acorns for hundreds of different types of forest creatures to store up and use during the harsh winters. His favorite types of trees were the sugar maples. These lush green trees were perfect for climbing and providing shade on a hot day. When he was young, his mother taught him how to tap the sweet sugar syrup from the maples for use in the house. Selling it had been a very nice source of income for the Bowmans. Now, neither Thomas, nor his father, were interested in tapping more than what they needed.

The trees had plenty of company. All around him he could hear the "teedle-eet" call of tree sparrows, the longer "chur-lee" of bluebirds, and the occasional twills and twitters of bright colored goldfinches. Thomas could see the peaks of the Appalachian Mountains rising just to the north and to the south. Its forest's and lakes provided plenty of trout and white-tailed deer for those who called the area home. Elden had taught Thomas at an early age to respect nature, so he was very good at recognizing different kinds of trees, birds, and other animals. If he needed to, Thomas could survive on his own for weeks.

SNAP! Thomas put his finger to his lips and

motioned for Ben to remain still.

Thomas carefully moved his rifle into a position where he could load quickly if he needed to. Anxiously he watched for a few moments. He was rewarded when a massive white-tailed buck appeared in a small clearing about one hundred yards ahead of him. Thomas quickly counted the points on his antlers. There were at least ten! *Ha!* Now there was a prize to brag about. The best his father brought home only had eight.

Thomas slowly began the loading procedure he could now do in his sleep. He carefully lifted his polished oxen horn with the Bowman **B** engraved on it and primed the firing pan with a fine layer of powder. After sealing the pan with the frizzen, Thomas used an attached hollowed horn tip to measure enough powder to pour down the barrel. Keeping his eyes on the buck, he then drew a greased patch, or piece of cloth, located in the brass patch box on the stock of the rifle. The patch helped give the ball a tight fit when the rifle was fired. With his other hand he drew out a lead musket ball from his haversack. The ball was seated in the center of the patch and then stuffed down the barrel with a ramrod, which was then replaced in its holder. All of this was done fluidly in the span of about twenty seconds. He cocked the hammer back as far as it could go and brought the rifle up into the ready position. The buck turned perfectly, giving Thomas the angle he needed.

Crash! Before Thomas could pull the trigger Ben had gotten his rifle tangled in some low hanging branches and in an effort to dislodge it he slipped and fell.

"You clumsy oaf!" Thomas saw the deer's head turn towards them and glare. Thomas had been hunting long enough to know what it meant when the buck's muscles began to tense. "No!" In a graceful bounce the deer dashed away.

Thomas was not about to give up on this one without a battle. Un-cocking the hammer he helped Ben up and bounded through the brush after the buck. He couldn't help but be impressed at the nimble movement of his prey. The deer vaulted over obstacles with ease, forcing Thomas to dodge a variety of hazards. He almost fell several times, tripping on roots and stumbling over dips in the forest floor. Finally the buck burst through a tree line into a wider clearing and was making a mad dash to the other side. Thomas could hit a moving target, but the deer was almost two hundred yards away now and getting farther with each breath.

He again pulled the hammer towards him as far as it could go, aimed, and fired. The jaws of the hammer snapped the piece of flint into the frizzen, sending sparks into the pan. With a flash and a "snap-boom" the rifle fired. Thomas could hear the echo rolling off the land around him. A group of sparrows dashed from a nearby tree, a squirrel scattered to a bush, . . . and he saw his target reach the other side of the clearing unharmed. "This just isn't my day." Thomas shook his head disgustedly.

Ben emerged from the woods panting. "Sorry, Thomas."

"Forget it, Ben" Thomas sighed. "The way things are going for me today I would have missed anyway."

"Not the way you shoot. You don't miss anything."

They were jolted by a crash from behind them and whirled around just in time to see no less than six more deer loping their way. One of them, a five pointer, careened towards Ben. The buck's eyes were bulging from its face as it continued on its collision course with Thomas's young friend.

Thomas reacted just in time. He raced over and threw Ben out of the way bringing up his rifle into a defensive position. The gun helped to absorb part of the impact but the weight of the buck slammed him to the ground. He felt a sharp pain and the air escape from his lungs as one of the buck's hoofs stomped into his stomach. The buck paid no heed to the human he had trampled. As Thomas rolled to his side, he watched the group of deer continue into the same clearing after the buck. Eventually, they too disappeared on the other side.

"Thanks, Thomas," said Ben regaining his feet first. "That deer had me in his sights. Are you alright?"

"I've had worse." Thomas mumbled brushing off his linen hunter's frock and matching tan breeches that were almost too small for him now. The rifleman's shirt was made with an opening in the front. His fingers gingerly probed his undershirt. The antlers from the deer had made a nice sized rip in the cloth. Thomas winced as he traced a slash-a result of the antlers. His fingers were smudged with his own blood. He knew it wasn't anything very serious, but it was definitely time to go home. Thomas gingerly moved his legs and arms to make sure they still worked and slowly bent over with a grunt to pick up his round felt hat that lay in the dirt. After inspecting the feather that adorned the top, he gave it a smack and flopped the hat back on top of his head.

"What would make them do that?" asked Ben.

Thomas was asking himself the same thing. The sound of his rifle should have made the deer run away from them not towards them. The only explanation for what they did was that something else scared them. Something they saw as a bigger threat. Thomas was not going to let them stick around to find out the source of that something.

"I think it might be time for us to start heading home," said Thomas.

Shadows crept through the trees, and now that the warm August sun had dipped below the horizon, Thomas felt a chill that he hoped was from the change in temperature. His hunter's shirt was what many men wore. It was perfect because it kept Thomas cool in the summer and warm in the winter depending on the number of shirts he had on underneath. When he started out it was warm. The temperature had now dropped several degrees. Thomas wished he packed an extra shirt because he started shivering. He took a minute to figure out exactly where they were and then headed east towards home. "Let's go, Ben."

After they had gone for a little while Ben stopped. "Something just doesn't seem right. Do you get the feeling that we are being watched?" asked Ben, worriedly looking into the woods on either side.

"It's just your imagination. Keep moving." Thomas also felt like they were being watched, but didn't want to alarm his younger friend. Without thinking he quickened his pace. He wanted to run. His hand clutched at his linen hunter's frock to protect him from the chill. Imagination or not, Thomas kept his eyes on both sides of the woods for any sign of danger and tightened his grip on the rifle. It was quiet. After minutes that felt like hours, he began to cross familiar landmarks.

"We are almost there," Thomas said reassuringly to Ben who was desperately trying to keep up.

Snap-Boom! The crack of musket fire erupted from the trees to their left. Thomas heard the zip of a ball and then a groan. He turned in time to see Ben fall to the ground, eyes wide with shock.

"Ben!" Thomas yelled, running over to his fallen mate. As he crouched over to check on him, Thomas sensed a presence behind him. He spun around and came face to chest with the most terrifying Indian he had ever seen. Almost twice his size, the brave wreaked of death and violence. A jagged scar ran the length of his muscular ripped chest and stomach. A wicked looking tomahawk was gripped in one massive paw, a smoking rifle in the other. The Indian tossed down his rifle and quickly grabbed Thomas's and flicked it away as if it were a toy. Thomas identified the signature streak of hair down the middle of the Indian's scalp. *Mohawk!* "Why?" he gulped as best he could. "We have done nothing to you. Why did you shoot him?"

The Mohawk leaned closer penetrating Thomas with his mean, bloodthirsty eyes. "You have done everything to me. Know that before you die I, Anachout, fight for the Six Nations that has declared war on your people."

The brave brought up his tomahawk poised to strike while Thomas remained still, unable to act, frozen with fear.

"Hold!" The Mohawk paused and glanced over to see who had interrupted.

Thomas recognized the source immediately, a mirror image of himself, only older. "Father!" Elden Bowman, brandishing his rifle in the ready position, moved closer keeping dead aim on the Mohawk.

"Move away, Thomas," commanded his father.

"What is the meaning of this?" Elden demanded of the Mohawk once Thomas moved a safer distance away. "We have no quarrel with the Iroquois. We have maintained peace in this area and trade freely with one another."

"Your peace is your own," answered Anachout

drawing a nasty looking scalping knife from a belt at his waist. "You are squatters. The Iroquois nations have joined in treaty with the Great White Chief in England; you and your people are, and always have been, the enemy."

Elden shook his rifle at the Mohawk, "I have stayed out of this fight, as has my son. Your fight is with others farther to the south."

The Indian's eyes narrowed, "My fight is with all who live on Iroquois land, my fight is with you!"

With incredible agility the Mohawk spun and viciously slashed at Elden with his tomahawk. Elden deflected the blow with his rifle. The Mohawk withdrew and looked for another opening to attack. Thomas grabbed his own rifle just as two more Mohawk warriors emerged from the trees, rifles poised and aimed at his father. Elden again directed his rifle at Anachout. They were in a deadly stand off.

Keeping a watchful eye on his opponents, Elden whispered back to Thomas. "Now you listen to me," he hissed. "I'll get away, but you have to go warn General Schuyler at Fort Ticonderoga that the British Army is moving in their direction. The rumors are true."

"How can you be so certain?"

"Look at the muskets those braves are holding. Brown Bess, standard issue for the British regulars. Not something I would expect to see Iroquois warriors carrying without British troops close by."

Thomas looked closer at the muskets the braves were holding, his father was right. "I'm not leaving you!" growled Thomas. "Or Ben."

"I think Ben is beyond our help, Thomas. There is no time to mourn or argue, just go! I'll meet you at the Fort."

Thomas still hesitated, not wanting to leave his father or his fallen friend in such peril. Again Anachout lunged in. Elden parried the Indian's tomahawk with his rifle and ducked under a killing blow from the brave's knife. The Mohawk smiled confidently; amused at the sport. Elden kept one eye on the massive man and again turned to Thomas.

"Now is not the time to be stubborn, *Move!*"

Thomas hesitated for a few more seconds. He

glanced at the other two Mohawks moving in, rifles still at the ready. His father was right. Someone had to go warn the garrison at Fort Ticonderoga that big trouble was on the way.

"Take care of yourself Father!"

"I'll be fine. I'll find you. I promise!"

Just before Thomas turned to run, Anachout gave a signal to the others. They were coming after him. Gripping his rifle tightly, he darted off the path he had been following and headed south through the woods.

He heard Anachout snarl behind him, "Enough of this, time to die land stealer." Whether that was meant for his father or him, it didn't matter. He was in a race for his life. *Good luck, Father!* Thomas knew he needed some, too.

2

Thomas sprinted through the trees, his pursuers close behind. If the Mohawks knew where he was headed they would surely stop him. Was his father right? Were the rumors true? Was the British Army behind these Mohawks, or was this something they had decided to do on their own? If he made it to the fort would anybody even listen to him?

Thomas needed to think quickly. Ticonderoga was about eight miles to the south. In order for him to make it, he was going to need to throw his pursuers off or find people to help him. He knew these woods as good as anyone. There was a collection of farms about three miles away. If he could make it there, he had more of a chance of surviving the night. The Mohawks chasing him had to know that, too.

Snap-Boom! As if to answer his thoughts, a musket ball rushed by his head and splashed into a tree in front of him. Snap-Boom! Another one zipped to his right and buried itself into the forest floor. As much as Thomas didn't like being shot at, he knew if they were stopping to shoot he could lengthen his lead.

Thomas cut a zig-zag path through the forest, making sure his eventual direction was south. He constantly had to scramble up and down slopes and ledges that could spell disaster for him with one missed step. He purposely dodged through small tangled junipers and redbuds to avoid getting hit, and to hopefully slow down the Mohawks following. The length of his rifle made this hazardous, but he still was able to move swiftly. He also had another ally, the night. It was now completely dark. Hitting a moving target they could hardly see would be difficult.

Snap-Boom! Snap-Boom! Two more balls sang by him, impaling harmlessly into the ground. His lungs ached for him to stop and catch his breath. He knew that option was out of the question. After a few more desperate moments, he saw light from a window ahead and smelled smoke from the chimney. He recognized the farm instantly. *The Chapmans! I made it!*

A scream eerily split the darkness followed by the

sound of small gun fire. *That came from the house*! Ominous shadows cast by lanterns from inside the home confirmed the worst. *More Mohawks!* He heard the discharge of another weapon. The screaming unmercifully continued, stopping him in his run for safety. The cut on Thomas's stomach ached from the encounter with the buck and his chest heaved, craving a chance to rest. Despite the possible danger he moved towards the Chapman home.

"Yeeea!" A Mohawk brave charged him from behind. Instinctively, Thomas turned and brought up his rifle to protect himself from the tomahawk that was slicing towards him. The stock of his rifle blocked the weapon and the rifle's momentum continued up, clubbing the Mohawk on the side of the head. The warrior dropped to the ground, motionless. For a few shocked moments Thomas stood there looking down at the Iroquois whose skull he had just cracked. Thomas had never killed another human being. Pulling himself slowly away, he crept closer to the house. This was not a time for regrets.

Thomas heard another scream from inside the house and sounds of more struggling. He heard a door open and close with a bang. Indian war cries penetrated the walls to the outside, churning his guts to mush. He pressed himself up against the side of the house and held his breath as he heard several footsteps leaving the front of the Chapman home. Instead of getting closer they thankfully grew fainter as their owners moved away from the house.

Thomas wanted to go inside and check on the family who had been neighbors all his life. *Don't be a fool! There probably isn't anybody left to help.* Thomas had no choice but to move past the farm and work his way towards another. He heard more screams and gunshots farther to the south. His father had to be right. There was no longer any question; Crown Point was under attack by an organized force. Ticonderoga had to be next. *Now what?*

Again Thomas pressed himself against the Chapman house. He could hear nothing coming from inside. Thomas realized what that meant. Like Ben, he would have to mourn them later. He heard footsteps again as he cautiously moved around the farm. Snap-Boom! Thwack! A musket ball smacked into the side of the house, missing his head by inches, and showering him with splinters. Whoops and war cries rang from all around. He had to move fast.

Thomas decided to change directions. Maybe instead of moving by land he could gain more speed by water. The Chapman farm was only a small distance from Lake Champlain, and he remembered they had a few small boats and canoes docked at the shore. *I might make better progress that way. Hopefully most of this Mohawk force is moving on foot.* It was a gamble he knew, but it was a chance he had to take.

He moved slowly down the path that he thought lead to the docks. A scream knifed through the air behind him. Thomas whirled to see a Mohawk racing toward him with tomahawk poised menacingly to strike. Thomas tried to bring up his rifle, but the brave kicked it out of his hands. Before he could slice at Thomas, a flash and a muffled snap-boom sent the warrior toppling to the ground.

Thomas turned to see a trembling young woman holding a smoking pistol. "Mary?" Thomas whispered. "Mary, is that you?"

"Yes, it's me," she sobbed, her body shaking.

Thomas moved closer and even in the dark, he could make out the unmistakable, blood-spattered face of Mary Chapman, the eldest of the Chapman's daughters.

"Thank you, Mary. You saved my life."

"I . . .couldn't . . .save . . . their's." she pointed to the cabin. "The Mohawks came out of nowhere," she wailed, her tears smearing the bloody evidence of the evening's tragedy. "They massacred them, my family, all of them!"

Thomas picked up his rifle, and pulled her with him. "I'm sorry for what happened to your family, Mary, but unless you want to suffer their fate, we need to get out of here now!" His statement was punctuated by a series of war calls that echoed through the darkness from several directions at once.

"Mary, does your family still have the boats docked on the lake?" he asked. Mary just stood silent as if in a trance. "Mary!" Thomas yelled again.

"Yes," she sniffed. "They should be there."

"We might have a chance to get away then. The lake may be our only way to escape. We have to get to Fort

Ticonderoga." He grabbed his rifle from the ground.

"The boats are down there," said Mary between sobs. She began heading down the path that he remembered lead to the water.

They were almost to the bank when Thomas saw a shadow of movement ahead of them. "Wait!" he hissed. Thomas pulled her into the woods that lined the path. "Look by the boats."

Mary followed his gaze to the wooden docks that contained the Chapman boats. There in the darkness was a Mohawk crouching down at the side of one of the canoes.

"What is he doing?" Mary asked.

"He is cutting the boats loose," Thomas hissed, "making sure nobody can escape through the water."

From every direction came screams and sounds of combat. Thomas knew they would be caught if they didn't move. First he had to stop the Mohawk by the boats before the Indian cut them all loose. Already three boats were floating away with the current. There was only one left, which the Mohawk was diligently hacking free.

"If he gets that last one loose we are finished!"

Thomas turned to see two Mohawks closing in on them from behind.

He quickly loaded his rifle. Even under this kind of pressure his movements were efficient. *I have to stop him!* Rifle loaded, he held it in the ready position. He took a deep breath to steady himself. He had never before shot at a human target. He thought of Ben and his father. Thomas zeroed in on the Mohawk by the water. The rifle slammed back on his shoulder after the flash and snap-boom of being fired, but his aim was true. Splash! The impact of the ball sent the brave tumbling into the water right next to the last canoe. Thomas was surprised when he felt the heat of a shot from right behind him. One of the braves that had been running towards them was now on the ground. Smoke poured from the pistol mounted with silver clutched in Mary's hand. She saw him looking at the pistol.

"It was my father's. I guess it is mine now." she said, her eyes watering again.

Thomas grabbed her by the arm. "Nice shot; now let's go! We don't have time to reload."

Mary and Thomas made their way down to the

remaining boat and jumped in. One slash from the hunting knife that Thomas carried sent them on their way. The pursuing Mohawk arrived a moment to late. He took a couple of steps into the water and then raised his musket.

Fortunately for them they were in an Iroquois birchbark canoe, very light and very fast. "Paddle!" he urged. No sooner had the words escaped his lips than a musket ball buried itself into the hull of their vessel, urging him to desperately dig his oar into the lake.

Soon there were shapes all over the shore. "Faster! Faster!" he urged Mary. The lake's current was flowing swiftly in the direction they headed, and their furious paddling soon bore them away from the Iroquois on the shore. The snap-boom of musket fire echoed from all around. Shots splashed in the water on all sides of them. As they raced along, gut wrenching sounds could be heard coming from both banks. They could see rising flames from several fires through the trees. Crown Point was being exterminated. Thomas wanted to empty his guts right in front of Mary, but he needed to be strong for both of them. *Ben, father, the Chapmans, how many more of our friends and family have died on this night? My father will get away. He has to.*

He heard Mary sniffling on the opposite end of the canoe. *How horrible this must be for her!* Thomas never knew what to say when people were upset. "You were very brave back there, Mary. Thanks again for saving my life."

She looked over at him sadly, her face smudged and stained. Thomas reached into his haversack and retrieved a small white linen cloth that he handed to Mary. He used the cloth to wipe down his rifle. Mary leaned over, dipped it in the water, and wiped her face clean.

"I remember my father telling me about the old days of when the Iroquois used to raid villages like this, but it hasn't happened in a long time. They have been peaceful until now. Why are they attacking people who are just trying to make a living? Why did they kill my mother and my sisters? They . . . took . . . their . . . scalps, why?"

Thomas shuddered at the fate of the Chapman family. He wished he could give her a good answer, but he couldn't. Going to war didn't seem as glorious to him anymore. "My father is right. I think the rumors of a red coat invasion are true. The British Army is to blame for stirring up the Mohawks."

She finished washing the tears and blood from her face and did her best to look tough. "I hate them all! If the British Army *is* behind this, I will make them pay for what they did!

"Well for starters, we need to get to Fort Ticonderoga to warn the army that trouble is on the way."

Mary chewed her bottom lip and paddled with a renewed determination. "*You* better paddle faster then!" she sniffed.

As Thomas helped move the canoe through the lake, he noticed the moon displaying its shimmering reflection in the water underneath him. Thousands of stars kept it company in the clear evening sky. The beauty contrasted the destruction and death around them. *Everything has changed now*, he thought.

Mary must have finally noticed the tear in his shirt. "Are you hurt badly?" she asked.

Thomas shrugged "Just a little hunting accident." he said sheepishly, pulling his hunter's frock over the spot on his undershirt. He didn't want her to know that he was almost trampled by a deer.

Thunk. Thomas heard what he thought was an oar striking the side of a boat somewhere behind them. Were they being followed? Snap-boom and Zip! A musket ball whizzed past his head to confirm his suspicion. Through the mist that was rising off of the cooling lake, he could make out at least five boats heading in their direction filled with determined Mohawk warriors.

"We might want to pick up the pace a bit!" he said rowing even harder.

Ticonderoga was built at the south end of the lake. They still had to paddle for a few miles to reach safety. The pair plunged their oars desperately into the water to get more speed. More shots sounded behind them. Zip! Zip! Balls splashed all around. One of them clipped his shirt and imbedded itself right in front of Mary's feet, making her yelp.

The Mohawks had more men to row and were gaining. Thomas had to slow them down. "Mary, keep paddling; if they gain too much ground, we are finished."

He tossed his paddle aside and grabbed another greased patch from the stock of his rifle. After rummaging through his hunting bag for another lead ball, Thomas loaded his rifle while seated and took aim at the closest canoe. Musket balls now began to hum by him with even greater ferocity.

The snap-boom from the rifle rocked the canoe, but his aim was accurate. The Mohawk it struck splashed into the water. Thomas had no time to think. He reloaded and shot again. Another splash confirmed his effectiveness.

Mary maintained their pace, and now more of the Mohawks took to their muskets trying to hit them. "Great job, Mary! with them shooting, we can gain a little ground."

"Unless they hit us!" quipped Mary as another ball whooshed dangerously close.

"Right!"

Thomas dropped his rifle and went back to paddling. His muscles strained with the effort of the wood against the water. Mary didn't even look tired. *If she can do it, I can do it!* His arms were screaming for him to stop, but he continued to dig faster and faster into the lake.

Just as his body was about to quit, he saw one and then several lights ahead. "Almost there!" He knew the lights came from the walls of Fort Ticonderoga. This would be cause for celebration if he didn't glance back to see that the Iroquois were again catching up. They still had a few miles to go.

Suddenly there was a high-pitched birdcall from the shore. *A signal perhaps?* The air that had been filled with the sounds of musket fire became silent. Thomas looked back to see the canoes were now heading to the banks of the lake. He and Mary were safe. *Why did they stop chasing us? They had time to catch up before we reached the fort.*

"We're going to make it!" said Mary triumphantly.

"I think we were *allowed* to make it, Mary."

She shrugged and gave him an appraising look. "You are quite the sharpshooter, Thomas."

"Killing people is not something I ever wanted to be good at." Thomas now realized it was one thing to hear stories of glory and combat, it was quite another to actually take another's life.

"Well, like it or not, you are good. I don't feel sorry for them one bit. They murdered my family." She had a point.

"Besides," Mary continued staring at the lights from the walls of the fort, "you kept us alive."

"For now, the night isn't over yet."

3

As they maneuvered to the dock in front of the fort, a commanding voice barked out, "Who goes there?"

Thomas quickly responded, "Thomas Bowman and Mary Chapman from Crown Point."

Two armed guards appeared by their canoe. The soldiers wore dirty, brown, regimental jackets marking them as Continental troops. Both of them had their muskets pointing straight at Thomas and Mary.

"What brings you two youngsters out at this time of night?"

Thomas didn't particularly like being called a youngster. "We have been attacked, sir, Mohawks, and lots of them. My guess is that the British Army isn't very far behind." The words came out in a rush. The soldier's eyes tightened at the mention of the red coats. He didn't seem convinced.

Mary had been silent but now spoke. "Please, sir, we need to see the officer in charge right away!"

"Do you now, lass. I'm quite sure General Balderdash has better things to do tonight," the officer responded, yawning dismissively.

"General Balderdash!" Thomas moaned. "Where is General Schuyler? I thought he was in charge here."

"The whereabouts of the general are not *your* concern, young man. But if you must know, the Congress in Philadelphia sent for him. General Robert Balderdash is in command until he returns. Now, you two love birds need to move along, or I'll have to send you back up the river with sore bottoms!"

The other soldier lowered his musket. He pointed at Thomas's ripped hunter's shirt and then toward a hole in the canoe's side made by a musket ball.

"Well it certainly appears you two have been able to find some trouble." He thought a few moments more. "I'll take you into the fort, but I can't promise that the general will see you."

Thomas wanted to shake the man to make him believe the urgency of the situation but decided better. He and Mary hopped out of the boat and were instructed to follow the path ahead of the soldier who still pointed his musket at them. The other soldier stayed by the water inspecting the canoe.

His father had taken Thomas to Ticonderoga before, but he was still struck at its perfection in design. The fort was a majestic structure rising out of the surrounding hillside like a castle. Ticonderoga was originally built by the French to protect their fur trade. It was named Fort Carillon. Once the British Army took control of it, they renamed it Ticonderoga after the village that lay on the east bank of Lake Champlain.

The fort had a rectangular shape, but was pointed at the corners to resemble a star. For further protection, an outer wall called a demi-lune was constructed in order to protect an approach from the east or from the south. These outer walls allowed defenders to shoot at an attacking enemy from several directions. The walls had first been built out of logs and mud but were later reinforced with stone from a local quarry. An attack from the north would have to come from the lake, which would be very difficult if the fort was prepared. To attack from the west an army needed to land and then move across ground that is covered by the fort's cannons the entire way.

Ticonderoga was strategically located at the junction of Lake Champlain and Lake George. It was here that the lake forked. To the west it became Lake George-to the east it continued on to the Hudson River. From the Hudson travelers could sail all the way through New York to the Atlantic. These waterways provided the most direct route from the colonies to Canada. There was no doubt that whoever held the fort had a major tactical advantage in the area. There would be no way of getting by on the water without controlling it. To punctuate this idea, several cannons lined the stone walls. There weren't as many as usual because quite a few had been hauled the 300 miles to New York City to aid General Washington's army months ago. Still, any force trying to sail past the guns that remained would be pounded to bits.

Cannons won't be useful unless there are men to fire them, thought Thomas. He saw a few soldiers patrolling on the tops of well-lit walls but not nearly as many as there should have been. Thomas could hear laughter and carousing from the inside. *These people are definitely not ready for an attack.* The soldier they were following guided them up a well-traveled path to a stone arch leading underneath the north wall. After a few feet, the three of them came to a sturdy wooden door. The soldier knocked and gave his name. Thomas could hear the clank of a lock from inside, and soon the big wooden door slid open.

A large soldier opened the door. He held a lantern and wore a tan jacket that failed to hide his massive belly. Thomas saw a green strip of cloth perched on the right shoulder of his coat, indicating some sort of rank in the army. A wisp of smoke rose from a clay pipe that he was holding. He held a half-empty bottle of alcohol in his other hand. Thomas and Mary were struck by the unwashed smell that seeped from his chubby body. The man looked annoyed at the interruption.

"So what is this, Anderson?" The plump man asked gesturing towards the two of them, "A couple in love, out for a stroll? Awful late for romance, son."

Mary sniffed indignantly behind him, "I have never

been so offended in my life! How dare you suggest such a thing! We need to see the general, *now*!" She stomped her foot and shook her fist at the guard. Mary's face had lost all trace of remorse that Thomas had seen when he found her. Even in the dim lamplight, he could see red coloring her cheeks.

The guard couldn't care less. "Oh really, just like that, huh," he asked. His face took on a mocking look, and he purposely puffed smoke from the pipe in her direction and took a swig from the bottle. "You may be a pretty little thing, but the general doesn't have time for the likes of you."

The soldier that had stopped them at the lake now leaned over to whisper something in the big man's ear. The guard regarded them again and let his eyes linger on the rifle Thomas clutched in his hand. "So you managed to get shot at by a couple of renegade Indians, did you? That's what you get for joy riding around the lake at this time. Go back where you came from, the general is busy!"

He was just about to slam the door when Thomas heard a voice boom from behind the guard, "Corporal

Dunston, what is going on here?"

"Nothing, Colonel, just a couple of children out causing trouble."

Thomas was fed up with being called a child, and from the looks of it, so was Mary. Still, he held his tongue to see what would happen next. The boyishly handsome man who came to the doorway was neatly dressed and wore a long, blue Continental jacket lined with red. The jacket had wood-backed buttons engraved with the letters USA. There was red ribbon attached to his tri-cornered hat signifying rank. He wore his hair braided in the back.

The officer took one look at the two of them standing in the doorway and gave Dunston a disapproving glare. "Look at them, Corporal! Do they look like they have been out having fun?"

Thomas realized what a sight he must be. After all of the day's events, he must have appeared like someone who hadn't bathed in months. He now felt very self-conscious in front of the well-dressed man.

"But, Colonel," the guard whimpered.

"Dunston, if you were half this determined to keep

food out of your mouth as you are turning away travelers, the whole army would be better off!" Thomas heard Mary snicker behind him.

The colonel turned to them. "My name is Colonel Joseph Cilley. Come inside and tell me what brought the two of you to Ticonderoga." Colonel Cilley turned and gestured for them to follow. "Dunston, if I catch you drinking on duty again, I will have your rank stripped from you faster than a hound to the hunt. And for God sakes, man, go introduce yourself to a bar of soap!" Thomas glanced back to catch withering scowls from both Corporal Dunston and Private Anderson.

The inside of the fort did not look like a military establishment ready for battle. Supplies were strewn over the ground, muskets were left unattended, and the cannon's artillery wasn't stacked and was nowhere near where it could be effective if needed. Thomas saw more than one man slumped against a wall, sleeping. From the sounds of the laughter of the men inside the barracks and the variety of empty bottles he saw on the ground, he knew they weren't sleeping because they were tired. The air was rife with the scent of neglect and abuse. The soldiers looked and acted like there wasn't an ongoing war when they should have been at their highest state of readiness.

Thomas must have had a sour look on his face because Colonel Cilley sighed disgustedly and grumbled, "Pretty pathetic isn't it? That's what happens when you let soldiers get lazy." Thomas figured a fort this important would always be battle ready.

I might have been able to conquer this place by myself!

"General Balderdash should be ashamed of himself for letting the fort get this way!" declared Mary.

"Well you are right about that, young lady," agreed Colonel Cilley. "Lately he has been so busy enjoying his command that he hasn't bothered with actually commanding. Fortunately, we have other leaders within these walls that still have an ounce of sense."

He led them to another doorway that opened into a small room. Colonel Cilley offered chairs to the two of them and found one for himself. "I'd offer you something to drink, but we haven't received supplies in quite a little while. I might be able to find some tea for you."

Thomas had been waiting about as patiently as he could, but his patience had run out. "That won't be necessary, sir. You are about to come under attack!" Thomas began relating the day's events to him. Colonel Cilley's lips thinned into a grimace at the mention of Anachout and the Iroquois, but his eyes nearly bulged out of their sockets when Mary told him what had happened to her family.

"Iroquois attacking farms, scalping women and children, why have we heard nothing about this?" Colonel Cilley jumped from his chair and began pacing around the room. "We haven't received any scouting reports about this aggression."

Thomas thought about that for a minute and then responded. "Colonel, when was the last time your scout reported?"

"Our last report was brought just moments ago by Private Reedy. He said there were some Iroquois in the area, but they were only a band of renegades that could be chased off by local militia."

"These were not renegades, sir."

Colonel Cilley considered the information. "I'm going to have to fetch General Balderdash. Maybe I should get General Arnold as well. At least we would have one commander in the room that might listen to logic. You two wait here; I'll be back."

"Thank you for your help, Colonel Cilley. You have been more than understanding." The Colonel fixed Mary with a sympathetic look and bowed gracefully.

"It is the least I could do after your ordeal on this night my lady."

After he left the room, Mary spoke up. "What a wonderful man! she squeaked. "I wonder if the colonel meant Benedict Arnold? I've always wanted to meet him!"

"I don't know of any other General Arnold," Thomas answered curtly. For some reason, the way Mary gushed over Colonel Cilley bothered him. "I thought he had gone south to fight with General Washington." Thomas tried as best he could to keep up with the events of the war from the scraps of information he heard at the farm.

"Mary, this probably isn't a very safe place for you.

I'm sure you could find someone to accompany you south to Stillwater; it must be safer there."

Mary looked insulted. "Oh, but it's safe for you to stay here. Just because I'm a *lady* doesn't mean I can't hold my own! I mean to make them pay for what they have done to my family!" Thomas thought that Mary was going to burst into tears, but she bit her quivering lip. "Besides it's always good to have a Chapman around."

"Silly *girl*, if you want to stick around and get your fool head shot off, then that's fine by me. Just stay out of my way!"

Mary's face reddened again, and Thomas thought for a minute she might slug him. Instead, she stuck a finger in his face and said, "Not only am I *not* going to get my head shot off, I am going to make sure you don't trip over your own feet and get *yours* shot off. I already saved you *once* tonight. Besides, it wasn't so long ago that my father pulled you out of the lake after you nearly drowned yourself. I think that's proof enough that you need us Chapmans around." Mary's eyes moistened again. "And since I am the only one left, it is now *my* duty to keep an eye on you!" She wiped her eyes with her sleeves and looked at Thomas.

Thomas was amazed by her resilience. Mary had lost everything yet still wanted to fight. He felt ashamed for speaking to her as he had. She also had a point. It was only about a year ago that he needed salvation from another Chapman. Thomas was fishing, and in his haste to reel in a nice sized brook trout, slipped and hit his head, falling unconscious into the water. If Mary's father hadn't been fishing a little farther down and dragged him out, they would have needed to "fish" his body out. That memory broke the tension between them. Thomas couldn't help but smile.

"I'm never going to live that down, am I?"

Mary had lost her edge too. "Nope, like I said, it's always good to have a Chapman around."

"I am sorry about your family, Mary," Thomas said with sincerity.

"I know you are, Thomas." She gave him a comforting pat on the arm. "But I intend to make some others sorry as well. They stole my family from me. I will see that justice is done!"

The door opened, and Colonel Cilley marched in followed by three others. There was no mistaking who two of them were. One was General Balderdash. Thomas remembered him from when he was recruiting for the attack on Canada. He was of average height with a pointy chin and sloping forehead that made his nose stick out. He was well dressed in the uniform of a general. He had on the same coat as Colonel Cilley, blue with the red facing, but was cut shorter. The jacket was done up with gilded brass buttons that had the letters **NY** engraved on them. His white waistcoat was buttoned and had a blue rib band worn diagonally across the heart. Thomas made a note to himself to have someone explain all of the different colors. General Balderdash wore a white wig that was short and curled in the back. At his side, he wore a sword and a scabbard that was intricately decorated. Thomas got the impression that this man liked being a general and liked people to know he was a general. He had the look of someone who expected to be obeyed, and right now he appeared very unhappy.

Thomas knew the second man was Benedict

Arnold. He had also seen him recruiting in Crown Point about a year ago. The major general was much shorter than Colonel Cilley and General Balderdash. His round face and smooth features made him appear to be a soft man. But his eyes were so intense, they seemed to jump from his skull. The General was wearing a coat similar to General Balderdash's, with the same white waistcoat. He had the same buttons attached to the jacket as Colonel Cilley, the intertwined **USA**. He also had a rib band that crossed his waistcoat, but his was purple and was matched by two purple armbands. General Arnold's light hair was short in the front and braided in the back. He smiled and made eye contact with everyone in the room. He winked at Thomas, who decided he liked this man right away.

Around his neck, General Arnold wore a silver piece tied by a ribbon. The silver was in the shape of a crescent moon and had a snake engraved on the front. The snake was broken into thirteen separate sections, with initials of the original colonies by each section. The words **"Unite or Die"** were engraved underneath the snake. General Arnold saw Thomas peering at the unusual piece of jewelry.

"It is called a gorget, a remnant from the days of armored nights. It helps remind me and others of what we are all about." Thomas thought he heard General Balderdash snort.

Thomas had no idea who the third person was who entered the room. He was about Thomas's height, but very thin, almost too thin. His eyes were way too large for his gaunt leathery face that was attached to a neck that stretched a little too far from the rest of his body. He reminded Thomas of a vulture. The man was younger than the two generals, but older than Thomas. He was wearing almost the same hunter's frock as Thomas, except that it had a fringed cape that was embroidered with a variety of symbols and pictures. He had on a cloth cap made of wool dyed red that hid his dirty brown hair barely visible underneath. He also carried a knapsack, indicating he was on his way out or just recently arriving. *Is this their scout?* Thomas wondered. The man had a very shifty look about his small, beady eyes and a nervous stance. Despite the unease that the rest of his body betrayed, the man's mouth displayed a half grin that seemed to mock everyone in the room at once. Thomas didn't trust him.

General Balderdash turned to Thomas and sniffed, "Well then what is it, stories of Iroquois war parties and the entire British Army? What else? Ghosts and Goblins riding in the night I suppose?" The younger man cackled at the comment. Thomas didn't trust the man, and now he didn't like him either.

"No sir, I . . . I . . . I mean yes, sir. I mean, I know what I saw, sir. They were acting too well coordinated for it to be just a group of renegades." Thomas felt like his tongue was twisted up in his mouth. "And they were using British Brown Bess muskets." It wasn't every day, or ever, that he found himself in the room with *two* generals. General Balderdash gave an indifferent wave of his hand.

"Brown Bess muskets," he announced every word as if they were a bad piece of meat. "Bah, how would a farmer's boy know anything about this sort of thing?"

"But General, sir . . ."

"My scout has reported nothing of this," General Balderdash snapped in annoyance. He turned to the younger man. "Private Reedy, have you seen anything while scouting to suggest a coordinated attack by the Iroquois and the British Army?"

The private was almost too anxious to respond. "My general, I just came back into the fort an hour ago and saw nothing to even remotely suggest what this, this ignorant farmer boy says."

General Balderdash patted the man on the shoulder. "You see, Private Reedy has been one of our most reliable scouts, and he sees no cause for alarm." Thomas decided if Reedy was a dog, his tail would be wagging now.

"I beg your pardon, General." General Arnold addressed Balderdash then turned to smile at Thomas again. "I'm curious to hear *why* he thinks the British Army is involved. Did you see any soldiers, young man?"

Thomas knew he couldn't give them the My-father-told-me-so routine, so he had to sell them on his own reasoning. *Please don't sound like an idiot!* he pleaded with himself.

"No, General, I did not." Thomas thought he heard Private Reedy make a disgusted sound. Benedict Arnold gave the private a look that warned him to keep silent. "You see, it's no small secret that the red coats have been negotiating with the Iroquois Nations for the last couple of years. It is also no secret that King George and Parliament are getting impatient for this war to end. It is well known that General Burgoyne has been given command of the British Army in the north, and he has bragged, to anybody that will listen, his intent to come down the Hudson. Who better to lead this attack then the Iroquois who know the land as well as we do? If this is just a bunch of renegade Mohawks, why did they attack every farm along the lake? It is because they want nobody left to warn you that the British Army is coming, and they want to eliminate resistance. When Mary and I escaped, they followed us. When we got close to the fort, they immediately went to shore even though they could have chased us down before we made it. Why? Because they didn't want to be noticed by the soldiers. The whole thing seems too well planned for it to be just coincidence. This fort is going to be attacked, and it's going to be soon!"

    Thomas impressed himself at how confident he

sounded. Here he was surrounded by two high-ranking officers, and they wanted to hear what he had to say. Well, at least one of them did. Mary and Colonel Cilley smiled proudly at him. Thomas didn't get very long to enjoy the moment.

"Rubbish!" General Balderdash proclaimed. "That is absolute rubbish! You expect me to move *my* army based on *that* bit of fantasy!" Thomas saw Reedy grinning like a man who had just found gold. "All you have brought to me, young man, is a bunch of guesses. Armies don't move based on guesses; they move based on fact. Have you *actually seen* any red coats?"

"Well . . . no I haven't, sir."

"Then I think that concludes this discussion. You two are welcome to stay for what is left of the night, but out you go in the morning. If you start working up my men about any of this, I will personally haul you out by your ears. Colonel Cilley, if there is nothing else; I will go *try* to enjoy the rest of my evening."

General Balderdash turned to walk out the door with Private Reedy right on his heels, but Benedict Arnold stopped him. "Excuse me, General. I do agree that we do not have enough to announce an alert at this time, but no harm could come from a little caution. May I suggest that we move a few men to the hills outside the fort to provide ample warning just in case young Thomas is correct?" General Balderdash looked like he was about to object, so Benedict Arnold hastily added, "Just a few men, General, nothing to get the others worried."

Balderdash gave Benedict Arnold an imperious stare and then shrugged his shoulders. "Alright, Arnold, if it will help you sleep well, we can send a few men *in the morning*! There will be no movement tonight. That would certainly get everyone asking questions."

Benedict Arnold saluted the general, "Thank you, sir."

General Balderdash gave a half-hearted salute and stalked out of the room. Thomas swore he heard him muttering the words "ghosts and goblins" before he left.

The tension in the room certainly eased as soon as General Balderdash and the disagreeable Private Reedy left. "I am indebted to both of you for your service to this army," Benedict Arnold said to Thomas and Mary.

"Do you believe us, General Arnold?" asked Mary.

"Yes, young lady, I do, but I am not in charge, so I do what I can. I am sorry to hear about what happened to your family. They will be remembered as heroes when this is all completed. This aggression towards women and children is troubling to say the least. And scalping? The British Army usually doesn't allow that sort of thing. Either the Iroquois *are* acting on their own, or the force that is headed our way is lead by someone more ruthless than we have ever dealt with."

Tears formed in Mary's eyes, compelling her to munch on her lip. "Whoever it is, I'm going to make them regret what they have done. You are most kind, General Arnold. Thank you for listening."

Benedict Arnold gave Mary a bow and extended his hand to Thomas. "Thomas, I will see you soon I hope. We always have room in this army for young men with wits like you."

Thomas was flattered by the praise. "Thank you, General Arnold, but I am here only to meet my father, and then I will return home. He should be joining me here soon." Thomas had enough adventure now to last a lifetime. All of a sudden, reading a good book at the Bowman farm didn't seem so dull.

"Very well. Colonel Cilley, See to it that these two have a warm bed to sleep in tonight. It will be morning soon. Good night to you." With that General Benedict Arnold left the room.

"That is a splendid man." proclaimed Mary.

"One of the best we have," echoed Colonel Cilley. "It's a testament to how great he is that he remains despite getting passed over for command. Both General Arnold and General Balderdash were major generals, but before General Schuyler left, he was forced to promote one of them to establish chain of command. General Schuyler picked Balderdash, promoting him to full general and by default, giving him command of the fort instead of General Arnold. Nobody has shown more bravery and cunning in battle than Benedict Arnold. Despite that, we keep getting stuck with men more concerned with image and politics than leadership. I would follow General Arnold anywhere."

Colonel Cilley may have said more than he intended because he quickly cleared his throat and motioned for them to follow. "Space is pretty limited, but I'm sure we can find decent enough accommodations for you two to sleep."

Thomas and Mary followed him out the door. After a few moments, he led them to another room that had a couple of cots and blankets. Thomas was exhausted after all that he experienced.

"Colonel Cilley, will you keep a look out for my father and spread the word to others to watch for him as well?"

"I will take care of it, Thomas. I'm sure he'll be along shortly." Thomas smiled appreciatively. "Oh, and don't let Private Reedy get to you. He *is* good at his job, but he needs to learn some manners."

"I don't trust that awful man one bit!" announced Mary, which was exactly what Thomas had been thinking.

"Well, I guess I can't blame you. However, right now he is the best we have." Colonel Cilley motioned to the cots. "I'm sorry I can't give you a separate room, Miss

Chapman. I know that is what is proper."

"That is understandable, Colonel. I am not offended in the least. Someone has to keep an eye on this boy," she said grinning.

"People better stop referring to me as a boy!" Thomas growled.

Colonel Cilley chuckled and winked at Mary. "You two get some sleep, no telling what tomorrow may bring." He set down the lantern he was holding and left the room. Mary's eyes followed him every step until he was out of sight.

Realizing Thomas had noticed her watching the colonel, she smiled at his discomfort. "Don't worry, Thomas, your father is very resourceful, he'll find us." Mary undid her linen cap and tossed it beside the cot.

For the first time since their frantic flight to the fort, Thomas took a good look at her. He noticed in the flickering light of the lantern she had changed from the little girl he, and his buddies teased growing up. Her face had matured. Big brown eyes with long lashes helped frame smooth tan skin and full lips. As a child, Mary had kept her black hair shorter; now with the cap removed, he saw that it had grown long. Mary shook her head to allow luxurious curls to fall just below her shoulders. She saw that she had Thomas's attention and smiled impishly. It took quite an effort for him to look away.

"I hope you are right," was all he managed to squeak out.

He reached into his knapsack to retrieve a new undershirt. Thomas tossed his rifleman's frock and shirt to the cot. He was just about to pull off the torn undershirt when he realized Mary was watching him. "Do you mind?" he said, embarrassed.

"Not *one bit* actually." she giggled.

Thomas walked across the room and extinguished the lantern. Now that the room was dark he quickly exchanged shirts. Before he plopped himself onto the cot, he heard Mary sigh.

"Oh, do grow up, Thomas!"

Even in the dark, he knew he was redder than an apple. *She's just a silly girl. What is the matter with me?* Despite his exhaustion, his emotions kept him awake for a while longer.

****

Thomas felt like he had just dozed off when he was jolted awake by an explosion. "What was that?" asked Mary sleepily from across the room.

"I think it was cannon fire." Thomas responded.

He was rubbing his eyes to try and get them to work properly when a second explosion rocked the room. Debris from the ceiling rained down. Mary screamed, and Thomas staggered over to grab her. It was a good thing he did, because when he reached the other side of the room, another blast shook the fort. Several wooden beams fell, flattening the cot he had been sleeping on.

Just then the door burst open, and Colonel Cilley rushed in. "Are you two okay?"

Although startled and covered with dust, it didn't seem like either one of them was hurt. "We'll live; what is going on?" Boom! Boom! As if to answer, more explosions erupted, and now he could hear men from outside yelling in confusion.

"Well, Thomas, it appears your ghosts and goblins have arrived, and they have brought their cannons with them."

4

Thomas grabbed his hunter's frock and rifle before entering into chaos. Men were running in every direction. Officers dressed hastily, screaming at soldiers to move this way and that. There was no sign of General Balderdash. Crash! Another round of solid- shot artillery struck one of the walls close to where Thomas, Mary, and Colonel Cilley stood, sending all three of them sprawling to the ground.

"We need to get out of here!" yelled Colonel Cilley. He pulled them to their feet and took off towards the southern end of the fort with Mary, hastily bundling her hair inside her cap. They sidestepped several bodies along the way.

I'd like to see Reedy's face now! Some scout!
"Renegade Iroquois, huh?" complained Thomas, hurdling over debris jarred loose by another direct hit.

The three of them rounded a corner and ran into a cluster of men huddled together. Benedict Arnold was in the middle. He was surrounded by others that looked to be officers by the various cockades, rib bands, and shoulder ribbons they wore, although a couple of them were still half-dressed.

"What are your orders, sir?" one of the men asked.

Despite the din of cannons that surrounded them, Benedict Arnold acted calm and commanding. "Well, unless the Iroquois have learned to fire and load cannons, it's definitely the British Army. I kept warning Congress that this was going to happen, and now it has." General Arnold said, knuckles tightening on the hilt of the officer's saber at his side. He released and took a deep breath to compose himself. "General Balderdash, left on the south road with Private Reedy and a few others. He is going to Fort Edward in order to establish a rally point." The look on Arnold's face betrayed his thoughts about how appropriate he thought General Balderash's actions were. "He has ordered us to withdraw from the fort and meet him there."

At this, one of the other men yelled heatedly, "Sir, we can still put up a fight here! Are we to give up the greatest fort in the north without a struggle?"

"General St. Clair, I appreciate your bravery. You know how much I love a good fight, but it is too late. They caught us by surprise." Benedict Arnold looked over at Thomas. They locked eyes and the general nodded slightly.

Why wouldn't Balderdash listen! thought Thomas disgustedly.

"They can pound us to bits from those hills, and I'm guessing their force is far superior to ours in numbers. There will be a time to fight back, but it won't be here. Our job right now is to save what is left of the army and the supplies. Here is what I want us to do. General St. Clair, we need to stall the advance of the attacking army. I need you and some men to use the cannons that are available to slow down any attempt at moving by the fort. If they try to use the water, make them regret it. When the moment arrives that you know you can't dally any longer, get yourself and the others out. I need you alive! Stay only as long as it is practical. I will organize the retreat. I mean to get every single breathing human being out of here safely."

General St. Clair saluted Benedict Arnold. "Consider it done, sir!" Thomas saw St. Clair grab a couple of soldiers that were close and point to the cannons on the top of the walls.

Benedict Arnold continued, "Once we begin our retreat south, we need a shield to protect us from attack. The red coats will try to finish us quickly. We don't have boats to carry us, so down the River Road we must go. Their officers probably figure we will have to travel by land, and *that* is the only road available. Colonel Cilley, I need you to set up flankers in the forest to watch for an attack from both the east and west. Once we move through the area, you are to cover our backs and protect the supply wagons and stragglers. We will all meet again at Fort Edward. Maybe there we will be able to turn around and give them better resistance. Good luck to all of you." General Arnold moved away with the others and began organizing the men.

Colonel Cilley looked at Thomas and Mary. "You two go with General Arnold. I'll see you at Fort Edward."

He turned to walk away, but Thomas stopped him. "Colonel Cilley, I'm staying with you. My father is out there somewhere. Besides, I know the land, and I'm pretty handy with this." He tapped his rifle.

"Thomas, I don't have time to argue, and you *are* of military age, so if you wish to stay with me, it is your choice. It will be dangerous. I have to organize the others. Meet me at the south gate." With that he hurried off.

Explosions still cracked the air, but the sounds of confusion had died down. Most of the soldiers and civilians Thomas saw were headed to the rallying point at the south gate with whatever they could carry. He could see General St. Clair on top of the north wall, screaming his orders to the few men he had recruited to stay. There was now an occasional burst of artillery coming *from* Fort Ticonderoga instead of only flying into it.

"You heard Colonel Cilley, Mary. You better get going." She gave him a look that could crack an iceberg.

"You are not in charge of me!" Mary growled. "If there is to be fighting, I mean to take part. I know how to shoot, too. Besides, I know the land just as well as you--if not better. I'm staying with you." She withdrew her father's silver plated pistol from her petticoat.

Thomas didn't know much about girls, but he knew

when an argument wasn't going to get him anywhere. "Do what you want, but I'm not responsible if you manage to get yourself killed!" With that he stormed toward the south gate.

Mary scowled at him for a moment and then followed. "You're the one that will probably need rescued, as usual!"

****

Benedict Arnold supervised as the army streamed though the south gate and out of Ticonderoga. The British Army's artillery blasts had slackened most likely to allow their troops to get close. Thomas hoped General St. Clair would be able to keep them back long enough. The last of the troops finally exited with Colonel Cilley's protecting their flank. He positioned his men in the woods to the left and right of the road in order to provide protection until the retreating army and local townsfolk could get by and General St. Clair could make his way out.

Colonel Cilley was not pleased at the sight of Mary

with Thomas, but a warning look from Thomas let the colonel know that there was no point in discussion. "Very well," he had said frowning at Mary. "You may stay with us and serve as an extra pair of eyes, but you are not to involve yourself in combat. Just to make sure we understand each other, I'll borrow this until we move on." Colonel Cilley snatched the silver mounted pistol Mary was holding. "It is against regulations for women to fight in the Continental Army."

Mary looked ready to throw a tantrum. "Well seeing how well you *men* have done so far, maybe the women *should* do the fighting!"

Colonel Cilley fought back a smile and cleared his throat. "Be that as it may, young lady, regulations are regulations. You may aid the retreat but only as an observer." Thomas thought he heard Mary mumble something having to do with stubborn men and oxen, but he couldn't be sure.

Colonel Cilley insisted that the two of them stay together, which suited Mary just fine. The colonel commanded about two hundred men. He spread them out in two thin lines on each side of the road to protect the retreating army. If an attack came, they had to hold at all costs, or the enemy could overtake those retreating. Thomas wondered what would happen if the British Army used the lake and sailed passed them in order to attack the retreating troops. If they did, the Continental's escape would be cut off.

The cannons from the fort eventually went silent meaning General St. Clair was going to try and make his move. If the British Army was sending an advance force by land, Colonel Cilley's troops wouldn't have to wait much longer to encounter them. Without cannons to oppose them, it would take only moments for the British Army to use the water to get by Ticonderoga. From there, the red coats could land and move to the south. If Colonel Cilley's men didn't slow down the British Army, the Continental's would be trapped in a bottleneck between Lake George to the west and Lake Champlain to the east.

As they waited in the forest, Thomas's heart raced. It was one thing to be thrown in the middle of a battle but quite another to wait for the battle to arrive. *Maybe they would be happy with just taking the fort,* Thomas wished to himself.

It wasn't long before his hope was dashed. Mary grabbed his arm and pointed up ahead. There was movement in the dark between the numerous oaks and pines, ghostly shadows making careful progress straight for them. The knowledge of impending battle and the uncertainty of the night helped to make the moment both terrifying and exciting to Thomas. Mary clutched at his arm to his right. She must have felt the same. "How did I get myself into this?" he muttered.

There was a flash and then a snap-boom. In that brief instant Thomas realized their assailants did *not* wear the red of the British Army. Another flash and another snap-boom! That was all he needed to identify the tell-tale hair style. *Mohawks!* More flashes lit up the forest. A series of Iroquois war calls echoed among the trees from ahead and behind. It sounded like they were going to attack both sides of the road leading south.

Thomas and Mary flattened themselves against a tree. Thomas fingered his rifle nervously. The sound of the war cries rose to a nerve-splitting crescendo. Thomas glanced behind him. The army had not fully retreated yet. He saw supply wagons surrounded by women, children, and men holding lanterns, still snaking their way down the road. Colonel Cilley's troops were going to have to stay and fight in order to let the others get through the area. From the movement up ahead and the sound of their war calls it wasn't going to be easy-they were badly outnumbered.

The continental soldiers opened fire illuminating the dark forest again. More shots followed. Sparks from muskets gave away the positions of soldiers defending the road. Mohawk Iroquois crashed through bushes and trees to close on their prey. The battle was joined. Thomas tried to distinguish target from tree, but it wasn't easy. Whack! Just as he was about to fire, a musket ball tore into the tree he was hiding behind and sent him spinning to the ground. "Bloody Hell!" he cried. An inch to the right, and he would have been finished.

"Watch your language! Do I need to hold you up?" scolded Mary crouched to his right. Thomas regained his balance and aimed at an advancing Mohawk. "Look out!" she screamed. Snap-boom! His rifle roared downing an advancing warrior. "Nice shot, but next time, don't wait so long!"

"Don't wait so long? Why don't you move south with the others where it is safe?" yelled Thomas. ZIP! ZIP! More shots whizzed around him, clipping the leaves and branches along the way.

"I'm not leaving without you!" shot back Mary.

Fool girl. Thomas continued to load and fire in an instinctive rhythm. Some of his shots missed, but many struck home. No matter how many Mohawks he cut down, there were more to take their place, and they were steadily gaining ground. It wouldn't take much longer before Colonel Cilley's men would be overrun.

Thomas glanced back nervously. Supply wagons were still making their way south. "They aren't going to make it!"

Thomas was so busy firing and loading that he had lost track of Mary. She soon appeared with a musket in her hands and a cartridge box slung around her shoulders.

"Where did you get that? Put it down! You heard what Colonel Cilley said!" Whack! Thomas ducked for cover again as a shot pounded a tree next to him.

"Don't be such a child! The soldier using this will not be missing it, and what the colonel doesn't know won't hurt him." Mary loaded and fired off a clumsy round into the trees, the force of the shot nearly knocking her off her feet.

"Do be careful! You're either going to get yourself killed, or your going to shoot me by accident!" admonished Thomas.

"It might not be an accident if you don't shut up!"

The Iroquois war party continued to press forward despite suffering numerous casualties. Hand to hand fighting had begun amongst the trees. Thomas could hear the clang of metal against metal.

Finally, Colonel Cilley screamed, "Fall back towards the road." This suited Thomas just fine. He and Mary began moving back the way they came staying as low as possible. A group of Mohawks emerged from the darkness and ran straight for them, tomahawks raised, desperate, crazed expressions on their faces. Thomas fired at them wildly, grabbed Mary by the arm, and took off in a dead run towards the road.

They were joined by other soldiers, but far less than the number that went into the woods earlier. Colonel Cilley organized a couple of columns to fan out across the road, blocking the path that the advancing enemy would need to take. He sent Thomas and Mary down the road to keep an eye on the last of the wagons. "We'll hold them up here as long as we can. Get those supply wagons moving!"

The two of them moved back to the wagons. The drivers were whipping at the draft horses as hard as they could to get more speed, but it was a lost cause.

"Yeeea!" Again, the air was split by a chilling series of screams. The Iroquois war cries began again. The horses pulling the wagons reared up, bucking against the direction of their handlers. The war cries continued to knife through the darkness from all sides. The drivers looked ready to jump off and head south without their cargo. Thomas couldn't blame them. At the moment, he wanted to run too.

From the road ahead, he saw a few soldiers

scrambling back. Private Anderson, the guard who had stopped them in front of the fort, was one of them. Thomas watched him, eyes wide with fright, running toward him. "I bet he believes us now!" The words had barely escaped his lips when Anderson screamed and plunged to the ground no longer moving.

Colonel Cilley and a few others gave up their defense and were sprinting down the road too. Just before they reached the spot where Thomas and Mary were waiting, Mohawks emerged from the woods on both sides.

The drivers of the two wagons near Thomas and Mary did not wait any longer. They hopped from their perches and ran desperately down the road. The Mohawks pressed the attack on the small amount of men still with Colonel Cilley. Thomas recognized one of the Mohawks immediately. He was *very* hard to miss. The deep scar attached to the immense muscular frame froze Thomas where he stood. It was Anachout, the same Mohawk Iroquois who shot Ben, and almost killed him.

If he lives what happened to Father? Thomas felt tears welling up in his eyes. Mary was frantically tugging at him to move, but it was as if he was watching a horrible nightmare. All along the road, hand-to-hand fighting continued between the remaining troops and the Iroquois braves. The huge Mohawk downed two soldiers almost at once and was about to finish them off with his scalping knife when he glanced up and noticed Thomas and Mary standing by the abandoned wagons.

Thomas was dimly aware of Mary screaming his name, but he couldn't move. The mammoth Mohawk's eyes were boring a hole straight through his skull. The Mohawk left the fallen soldiers on the ground and began stalking toward the two of them.

"What did you do to my father?" Thomas screamed in anguish, bringing up his rifle to fire. Anachout smiled menacingly.

"No, Thomas, we have to run!" Mary pleaded. The Mohawk seemed completely unfazed by the weapon pointed straight at him. He continued to walk directly toward Thomas. Thomas couldn't focus. He was lost in a haze of grief.

Snap-boom, Thomas fired. At the last moment, the

brave moved to avoid the ball that blazed from the rifle and closed the distance between them. With a crushing blow from his hand, he sent Thomas spinning to the ground. "You will not escape the knife twice!" He menaced from above, reddened blade inches from Thomas's scalp.

"Oh, no you don't!" Mary screamed as she swung the stock of the musket she was holding at the beastly Mohawk's head.

Anachout turned in time to block the blow with his hand. He, then, viciously jerked the musket free from Mary's grasp, and hurled it contemptuously to the ground. The Mohawk let go of Thomas to advance on Mary. She backed up as quickly as she could, but the brave was faster. He grabbed her by the hair, raised his scalping knife as he sneered into her face.

"You think you can stop me? Nothing can stop me! I am the Earth Mother's Avenging Angel!" he growled rearing back the knife to end her life.

Crack! Splinters of wood showered Mary. The brave released her and toppled to the earth like a fallen oak. "He's a big one!" exclaimed Colonel Cilley who stood over

Anachout holding the remains of a musket.

"Is he dead?" Thomas groaned, holding his own aching head.

"I doubt it," answered Colonel Cilley tossing away the shattered musket. "I'm not sure what it will take to finish that one." Thomas groggily regained his feet and began reloading his rifle. He wanted to avenge his father.

"No Thomas! There isn't time. We must run!" Colonel Cilley grabbed Thomas's rifle and shook it. The immense Mohawk began to stir at their feet.

Zip! Zip! Zip! Musket balls whipped past them, and several Mohawk warriors were closing fast. "Thomas please!" begged Mary. Reluctantly Thomas stopped loading, tugged his rifle away from the colonel, and nodded.

Thomas, Mary, and Colonel Cilley sprinted down the road. They passed several abandoned wagons along the way. At first there were sounds of pursuit, but they faded the farther the three of them moved. From the sounds of celebration behind them, their enemies were satisfied by the damage they had already done. As Thomas sprinted with his companions deeper into the night, he wondered if he would ever stop running.

5

They ran on in silence for about a mile and then slowed down. Morning had finally arrived. The sun was fighting with the trees to shine light on the road they were following. Thomas hadn't had much time to consider what had happened over the last day, but now his mind and emotions began to work furiously. The result wasn't pleasant.

The encounter with Anachout brought out Thomas's worst fears about his father. He doubted that particular brave would be easy to escape from. *He is dead. What am I going to do now? I'm alone.* He glanced over at Mary and realized she was struggling with the same feelings. As bad as Thomas felt, it couldn't be half as bad as Mary. Even *if* his father had been killed, at least he didn't watch it happen. Mary had witnessed the destruction of her family and home life with her own two eyes. Thomas wanted to walk over to her and comfort her, but he was unsure of what to say.

Mary had stopped and was seated on a fallen oak trunk that was alongside the road. She was crying. As tough and brave as she acted, she could only take so much. When Thomas's mother and sister had become ill, he at least had time to prepare himself for the possibility that they wouldn't survive. Mary was never given that chance. *I have to go say something,* Thomas thought.

Before he could reach her, Colonel Cilley stood in front of him. "Let her go, lad. She needs some time to herself. You two have been through a lot in a short amount of time."

Thomas had to gulp down his own tears. "I don't think my father made it. He was all I had left. I'm not sure what to do now." He didn't want to sound like a little boy, but he was tired, physically and emotionally.

Colonel Cilley gave him an understanding pat on the arm. "This war has been hard on all of us. I lost a lot of very good men. Sometimes I wonder if it is all worth it." he said, staring behind him at the road. "You can stay with us as long as you like, Thomas Bowman. I saw you with that rifle in the woods. We could use your help."

Thomas nodded his head in agreement. "Thank you, Colonel. I'll do whatever I can." Like Mary, he too wanted to punish the men responsible for his loss. "I need to make sure she has somewhere to go." Thomas said gesturing toward the still whimpering Mary.

Colonel Cilley smiled, "I think, Thomas, that she will go wherever *you* go."

They stood together for a few more moments and soon were joined by Mary, who had done her best to wipe away the tears that stained her cheeks. "So, what is next, Colonel?" Mary said, doing her best to sound brave.

The Colonel grabbed a stick and made a straight line through the dirt. "We need to continue on and meet up with the rest of the army. We will be at Fort Edward within a few hours." He said indicating a spot further along the line he drew. "From there a decision will have to be made as to whether we retreat or stand against the force headed in our direction."

"I'm tired of running," Thomas said defiantly. He was pleased to hear Mary agree with him.

Colonel Cilley looked at the two of them

thoughtfully and tossed the stick he was holding. "So am I, Thomas. However, there is a time to run and a time to make a stand. The trick is knowing when to do which. I might as well give this back to you, young lady," Cilley said withdrawing Mary's silver-plated pistol from his haversack, "You seem determined to get involved whether I keep this from you or not."

"Very determined," she replied stuffing the pistol somewhere within her clothes.

They continued to move down the road. Mary nudged herself between Thomas and Colonel Cilley. "Are you as hungry as I am?"

Thomas had forgotten all about his stomach. It had been a long time since he had something to eat. He almost wished she hadn't reminded him because now his stomach began to rumble.

Colonel Cilley either heard Mary's question or Thomas's complaining belly. He handed them each a piece of what looked to be hard cooked dough from the haversack at his waist. "It's called a fire cake; it's not much, but it will do until we meet up with the rest.

Hopefully, they will have something better for us."

Thomas took a hesitant nibble. "Not exactly roasted lamb, but it's better than nothing, I guess."

"Are you sure about that?" complained Mary staring at the fire cake like it was trying to bite her.

Thomas took a swig from his wooden canteen and handed it to Mary to help rinse down their meager meals. "What do you plan on doing once we get to the fort? My Uncle Morgan lives a few miles to the east; I'm sure he wouldn't mind if you stayed with him and his family for a while."

Mary gave Thomas an appreciative smile. "Thank you for the offer, Thomas, but I mean to see the men pay who are responsible for murdering my family. If I have to stay with the army to see that it gets done, then fine. I'm sure they can find something useful for me to do. Men can't do everything themselves, and it is *always* good to have a Chapman around."

"Moving with an army is no place for a fine young lady as you." said Colonel Cilley. "I'm not sure how my superiors will react to your presence."

Mary sniffed, "I am perfectly capable of taking care of myself, Colonel! You let *me* worry about your superiors. They need me whether they know it or not." She said crossing her arms. Colonel Cilley put his hands out in front of him in submission.

Thomas grinned. Growing up, he had thought of her as a nuisance, sticking her nose into his business, starting arguments with him whenever she could, acting like a typical, annoying girl. Now he respected her. She had been through something that would have made other's want to quit. She wanted to fight.

"Well, Mary, if you change your mind, the offer holds. I'm sure my uncle could keep you busy."

Mary was about to snap off a nasty comment and then thought better of it. "That is very kind of you, Thomas. You aren't the same boy who liked to throw grass in my hair." They shared a smile. "Are you going to stay and fight?"

"I don't really see any other option. I argued with my father for the longest time to join the revolution, and now I have my chance. It seems I too am looking for a little revenge."

"Not revenge, Thomas, justice! Revenge is for fools, justice is for the prudent," lectured Mary. "Besides, your father is a tough man who knows his way in a fight and in the woods. Until you are completely sure he is gone, don't give up hope. Sometimes hope helps to keep us going. If he is still alive, the army is the first place he would look."

Thomas knew she was right. For now, staying with the Continental Army was his best chance of protecting Mary, finding his father, and seeing that justice was done.

As they continued to move south, Thomas figured it might be a good time to ask the colonel about what the different colored sashes and patches meant on the Continental uniforms.

"Right now the regulations change about as much as our commanders. General Washington is trying to get things organized, but it is taking some time. We hardly have enough money for ammunition and supplies, so uniforms are not a major concern. As of now, General Washington has made the brown coat regulation, you may have seen a few of the soldiers wearing them in the fort." Thomas remembered what the men wore by the lake. "The blue coats that the officers have are from old regiments. I would guess that eventually these may become regulation, if we last that long. One good thing General Washington has done is come up with a system of recognizing officers. He stole most of it from his days with the British Army. Corporals wear a green stripe called an epaulette on the shoulder, and sergeants wear a red one. Captains have a yellow ribbon called a cockade on their hat, and colonel's a red one." He tapped the top of his hat that displayed the red. "The generals wear different colored rib bands. Did you notice that General Balderdash wore a blue rib band?" Thomas nodded. "That means he is the Commander in Chief of this army, a step below Washington who is the commander in chief of the entire Continental Army. Technically, he shouldn't be wearing it, but General Schuyler placed him in charge when he left, and General Balderdash took that to mean the right was his. General Arnold is a Major General so he wears a purple rib band and matching armbands. He should have been the one

General Schuyler placed in charge, not Balderdash, but the Congress thinks Arnold is too reckless." Colonel Cilley gave a disgusted kick at a rock lying in his path. "Anyway, the colors are not a bad system since we really don't have uniforms right now."

"The uniform doesn't fight, Colonel; it is the man inside that does." offered Mary as she smiled at him.

Colonel Cilley sighed and shook his head. "Quite correct, Mary. But this army lacks confidence and pride; you would be surprised what a clean shirt can do for someone. I have heard that some day General Washington will issue a general order to organize the uniforms better. Right now he is just trying to stay alive like the rest of us."

They walked for a few more hours along the river road when somebody commanded, "Halt!" from the woods. Six soldiers stepped out of hiding, bayonet-tipped muskets held ready. As soon as they saw Colonel Cilley they relaxed.

General St. Clair was next to pop out of the trees. He walked over and gave the colonel a hardy handshake and returned his salute. "It is good to see you well, Colonel.

Where are the rest?"

"I'm afraid this is the rest, General. We barely made it away ourselves. If you hadn't slowed up the advance a little with the cannons from the fort, this army would have been destroyed."

General St. Clair looked grim at hearing the fate of the rest of Colonel Cilley's troops. "If it wasn't for *your* heroic efforts, Colonel, the retreat would have been a complete disaster. It was bad enough anyway. Where are the rest of the supply wagons?"

"Suffering the same fate as the rest of my men," answered Colonel Cilley dejectedly. "The Iroquois must be the British Army's advance unit, a very effective one."

General St. Clair sighed, "We were undersupplied before the attack, now we are in serious trouble."

Is there ever any good news? Thomas thought.

"Well, General, we aren't going to have a whole lot of time to worry about it because unless I miss my guess, the British Army is not very far behind the Iroquois. A fight is coming if we have the courage to face one."

"I can't fire courage at the enemy," grumbled

General St. Clair. "We need artillery and soon!"

As Thomas listened a thought occurred to him. He cleared his throat tentatively. "Excuse me, sirs." The two officers turned their attention to him. "It strikes me as odd that the British Army has not made use of the lakes for transportation. All they would have needed to do is sail their forces around the fort in order to get ahead of us. They could then easily trap us between themselves and the Iroquois." Thomas definitely had their attention now. "Since they *did not* do that, we can only assume that they *can't*. Therefore, their only avenue to attack us is down the road we just came. It is the only one large enough to handle the wagons and artillery pieces that an army would bring with them." Thomas crossed his arms and smiled at the two men as if he had just solved a riddle."

"So what is your point, Thomas?" asked Colonel Cilley.

"Well, sir, there's no reason why we should make it bloody easy for them!"

"Thomas!" gasped Mary. "There is no excuse for that kind of language."

"He is absolutely right," admitted General St. Clair. "A few hours laying about with axes, and we can clog up this road but good." He patted a towering Cedar tree to emphasize his point. "If the British Army can only use the road, it would take hours to get their army through here to attack us. By then we can either be gone or be ready!" General St. Clair walked over to a few of the other soldiers standing nearby and must have given an order because a couple of them sprinted off right away.

Colonel Cilley gave Thomas an approving look. "I told you we could use you around here."

Thomas felt Mary give him a pat on his back, her fingers sending a tingle up and down his body.

"Good thinking Thomas, although next time don't curse." Thomas rolled his eyes.

St. Clair rejoined them a few moments later. "You three head to the fort, it is only a few more miles down the road. Our provisions are scarce, but we can at least feed you a little."

Thank goodness! Thomas thought.

It was late in the day when they finally encountered

small homes and shelters, letting them know that the fort was near. Soon it came into view. Fort Edward was nothing like Ticonderoga. It looked like whoever had built the place did so in a hurry. The walls were ready to collapse on their own, and everything else appeared uncared for in years. Thomas wasn't sure if it had ever been in good shape. *It definitely isn't now. What a wreck!* "Colonel Cilley, are we actually going to fight the red coats here?" Thomas asked.

"That is for General Balderdash to decide."

"Great! We're doomed!" spat Mary dispiritedly.

Colonel Cilley fought back a grin and cleared his throat. "We shall find out soon enough."

As soon as they entered the fort, Colonel Cilley sent a private to go find them something to eat and drink. Thomas saw a bunch of men head out of the fort with felling axes and ropes. If the men did a good enough job, the British Army would indeed have a tough time traveling down that road. The three of them found empty ground to sit; Mary plopped herself almost on top of him.

A couple of scruffy looking soldiers brought them

food and water. Salted beef, though not a feast, was much better than the fire cakes. As he munched on his meal, Thomas saw General Benedict Arnold approach, behind him a scowling Private Reedy. Thomas was surprised not to see him leashed to General Balderdash like a house pet. *In fact*, Thomas thought, *where is Balderdash?*

"I am glad to see the three of you are well. Colonel Cilley, I am saddened by the losses of your men. They are heroes to the cause. Their efforts may have saved this army for the time being. Thomas, I hear that once again you have offered wise advice. Colonel, we may have the making of an officer here."

Thomas blushed at the compliment and couldn't help but look at Private Reedy for his reaction. The private just glared at Thomas with a look of contempt.

"With any luck it could take days for the British Army to get untracked on that road." said General Arnold wiping his brow.

Colonel Cilley swallowed a bite and then asked, "Sir, do we mean to stand and fight here?"

Benedict Arnold shook his head. "No, Colonel, this

was just an opportunity to rally our forces together. We have been instructed to head south to Stillwater, New York. That is where we will unite with General Balderdash."

"General Balderdash is not here?" By the look on Colonel Cilley's face it was plain he was outraged.

Private Reedy was the first to answer. "No, the esteemed general and commander thought it would be best for him to see to our defenses in Stillwater."

"Where he's nice and safe. Some leader," muttered Thomas.

Reedy must have overheard him because he snarled threateningly at Thomas. "Silence, boy!"

Thomas wanted to get up and deck the nasty scout, but thought better of it.

"If we are to defend at Stillwater, General, why are so many still here?" asked Colonel Cilley.

"Our supply situation is desperate. Almost everything was lost in the retreat from Fort Ticonderoga. We may be able to get provisions from Albany, but they may not arrive in time. We have learned that we might be able to pick up supplies from the town of Bennington, in the Hampshire Grants to the southeast. It is very close to Stillwater. In a few moments a regiment will leave to secure provisions and bring them to our defenses. The rest of the army will remain and do what we can to block up the road. Hopefully, if we buy enough time, we can supply Stillwater and set up for a fight. Private Reedy will be moving out to find out exactly what we are up against. The only thing we know for sure right now is that the Iroquois are being used as an advance force. We have no idea how many British soldiers are behind them."

    Reedy again wore a smug grin that made Thomas feel like he was playing a prank. "I will be happy to provide you with that information, General." he purred.

    Thomas was very familiar with Bennington and the Hampshire Grants. They lay at least two days away and were situated on the east side of the Hudson River. His Uncle Morgan lived very close by. Thomas had visited him often with his father. It may be possible that he may have gone there once Ticonderoga fell to the British. *Maybe he is there. He could still be okay. He is too bloody stubborn to die!*

Thomas finished what he was eating and asked, "General Arnold, if it is acceptable to you, I would like to join them. I have visited the Grants many times and may be able to help show the way. Besides, I'm hoping my father is there." General Arnold didn't hesitate to approve of the idea. Reedy rolled his eyes and muttered something under his breath about farm boys.

Thomas expected Mary to ask to go as well, but she didn't. Instead she told Thomas that she would meet up with him in Stillwater. "I think I might be more of use here; besides I am a little tired of trudging around in the woods."

"Thomas if you mean to go, you better report to General Stark right away. He is the one leading the force to the Grants." Thomas got up and began to rush in the direction that Benedict Arnold had indicated.

Mary's voice stopped him. "Take care, Thomas. Don't trip over yourself. You don't have a Chapman to watch your back."

"I'll be just fine. You have fun sitting around in Stillwater," he answered a little sharper than he intended.

"I will not be just *sitting around!*" she replied,

crossing her arms defiantly. As Thomas left to find General Stark, he looked up to see the rapidly darkening sky. A whole lot of rain was heading their way.

6

General Stark was in his forties with a face that looked worn and older. He was an experienced soldier and woodsman who had fought in the war against the French. The general was more than happy to have Thomas along to help guide the men.

As it turned out, General Stark was also from the Hampshire Grants. The Grants were a rather large patch of land that separated the Hudson River from the Green Mountains. The people living in the Grants had recently declared themselves the independent state of Vermont and commissioned Stark to protect the area since they were losing faith in the army under General Balderdash. The supplies the Continentals needed were in the town of Bennington that was within the Grants.

The path to the Grants would be tough for people who hadn't traveled there before. The area was covered by thick forests, crisscrossed by hundreds of streams, and the rocky land would tire the hardiest of mountain men. The steady deluge of rain didn't help the trip either. Thomas hoped it would stop when they eventually moved on to Stillwater because it would be difficult to move supplies through the area in this kind of weather.

General Stark's command consisted of nearly one thousand troops, most of them militia. He positioned Thomas out in front of the main body so he could scout the land and guide them along the right path. It took several days to move southeast through the damp tangle of bushes and trees because of lousy weather, but eventually they made the outskirts of Bennington and the Hampshire Grants.

As Thomas rested in a tent, he wondered if his Uncle Morgan was nearby. He was his mother's brother, and Thomas loved spending time with him. Uncle Morgan was always willing to teach Thomas about hunting and how to survive in the forest. He hadn't seen him recently, but he had heard that his uncle was a colonel with the New Hampshire Militia that was active in the area. Thomas hoped he would run into him while in the Grants. Before sleep rescued him from his weariness he noticed the rain had stopped. *It's about time!* he complained to himself.

The next morning the army began to gather the supplies. General Stark moved his troops into the town of Bennington where they could load the wagons. Thomas tried to find his father, but he didn't have any luck. Nobody had seen him. Again, the knot in his stomach tightened thinking about what may have happened.

Frustrated, he turned his energy to helping the army load supplies, but got the impression he was in everybody's way. After a few hours of feeling completely useless he decided to head north into the woods around the town to do some hunting. With any luck, he could bag a few meals. *Anything has to be better than those fire cakes.* Just the thought of them made him grimace.

Thomas made sure that he didn't move too far away from where the army was, but he knew if he was going to have any luck hunting, he had to get away from the smell of humans. He would be lucky to find a half-starved rabbit with the racket going on in town. Thomas moved about a mile to the northwest and stopped. Finding a spot that provided him with a good hiding place, he sat and waited.

Even laying still, the August heat soaked Thomas under his hunter's shirt. He removed his feathered felt hat to wipe the drops of sweat that were trying to reach his eyes. *I don't know how people in the southern colonies can stand it!* He tried to see through the numerous pines, maples, and oaks to figure out the location of the sun. Thomas didn't want to stay out there too long. It was easy to lose track of time when hunting. *I'll stay just an hour, no more.* The woods didn't appear much different than the hunting ground by his house. There were a few more red oaks, but the calls of the sparrows and goldfinches were familiar. The thought of home made Thomas think about his father. *He can't leave me! He has to be alive!* Thomas clutched his loaded rifle a little tighter and watched the area out in front of him.

He was soon rewarded when a nice sized doe moved hesitantly out in front of his view. *Certainly no trophy, but having venison to eat will be prize enough.* Thomas focused on his target and was about to fire when he heard a snap of twigs from beyond the deer. Of course, the doe heard it too and leapt off through the protection of the forest. *It's a good thing I don't have to rely on hunting for food all the time!* "Nothing is ever easy!" he griped to a pair of brown thrashers that were sitting on a nearby dogwood branch. The thrashers finished grooming their striped underbellies and flew off with a series of chirps. "Thanks for the help." Thomas mumbled. He returned his attention back to where the deer had been standing.

Snap. Snap. Snap. At first he couldn't see anything other than the greens and browns of the forest. That changed a few seconds later when he noticed men cautiously moving between the trunks of the trees. The men carried muskets and wore…red coats. *The British Army!* his mind screamed. There was no mistaking the jackets and their bearskin hats. *Grenadiers! What are they doing here?* The British Grenadiers were carefully picking a path straight for the spot where Thomas lay hidden. If he didn't move soon, they would either see him, or trip over him. Either way it wouldn't be good. *Calm down and think!* His hand moved to the trigger on his rifle. *Don't be a complete fool! I may be good, but I'm not that good!* He had to get back and warn General Stark.

Snap. Snap. Snap. More and more shapes were warily sneaking towards him. At the front of the troops, Thomas could just barely make out a short skinny man acting as a guide. *That hat looks familiar.* He couldn't quite make out the man's face yet. *Come on, move a little closer. It looks like . . .* Thomas shook his head as if to get rid of something that had fallen between his ears. *I'm just imagining things; it couldn't be Reedy, could it?*

Thomas couldn't wait around to find out for sure. Within seconds the British Army would be on him. He had to make a run for it. Clutching his rifle, Thomas took every precaution he could to back away from the advancing force. He was so busy watching the danger in front of him that he forgot about the danger that might be below. In his haste to get away, his moccasins caught on a gnarled root of an oak tree and he slipped on the muddy forest floor. Thomas tumbled loudly to the ground. *Now I've done it!* He heard someone bark an order and the crunching of feet on the forest floor.

Thomas didn't care how much noise he made now. Thomas took off, rifle in hand, and dashed towards General

Stark and Bennington. As soon as he sprinted away he heard someone yell for him to stop and then the snap-boom of a musket. Smack! The lead ball splashed into a tree right next to him. *Whoa!* His heart pounded through his coat, and his feet raced over the slick ground. Another slip and he would be overcome by the pursuit he knew was closing in. Hurdling rocks, slamming through puddles, and zigzagging through the trees, Thomas avoided giving the men behind him a clear shot. With his body heaving to recover, he emerged from the woods and made his way towards the center of Bennington.

 General Stark and the rest of his command must have heard the muskets, because they were already in motion when Thomas came upon them. The general saw a muddied Thomas crash from the woods and was the first to confront him. "What in the devil is going on?"

 "Red Coats, sir, Grenadiers, and lots of them. They are heading straight for us!"

 "How in the devil did they know we were here?" General Stark said looking around. A defiant look shone in his eyes and he pounded his fist into his hand. "Well, no matter, we haven't finished gathering supplies, and we can't leave them for the British Army. It looks like this time we will have to put up a fight."

The general positioned his men throughout the town. Being a hunter himself, he understood the advantages of fighting behind cover. The troops quickly moved behind buildings, fences, and any other obstacles they could find to help protect them from musket balls. They moved just in time. Thomas heard the rhythmic roll of drums in the woods meaning the grenadiers were forming their lines inside the cover of the trees. He figured within moments they would move in unison towards General Stark's troops on the village green. He was right. Stepping with determination and confidence, the red-clad grenadiers moved from the cover of the trees and began their advance on the Continentals in town.

General Stark gave the command, "Open Fire!" and with a booming chorus of muskets the battle for Bennington began.

Thomas positioned himself behind a wagon and started picking targets. It was just a few days earlier that he felt horrible after killing an Iroquois brave. He had killed far too often since. *Better them than me.* That idea still didn't make him feel any better. He set himself through the paces of loading and firing. His father warned him about trying to shoot rifles too quickly. They were extremely accurate, but they would back up and become useless if loaded in haste, or as his father would put it, become a flash in the pan. Feeling inside his rifle bag, Thomas discovered he was also low on ammunition. *I should have made more before I went hunting!* He would have to make every shot count.

    The British Army was closing in; Thomas estimated they were about one hundred yards away. The snap-boom of musket fire resonated throughout the town. The din of the battle could probably be heard for miles. Hot air swirled with smoke from the weapons. The burning smell of powder came from everywhere. It made the adrenaline in Thomas's body erase any thought except battle and the enemy in front of him. Most of the targets he chose dropped to the ground and didn't move again. He almost felt sick from the deadly accuracy that his rifle possessed.

Thomas picked a good spot with an excellent angle on the advancing British Army, and there was very little of him for the enemy to hit. Most of the shots directed his way zipped harmlessly by him. With his blood pumping faster than he could have believed, he continued to fire away.

At first the battle went very poorly for the British Army. They were having a hard time striking an enemy that was so well protected behind buildings and other obstacles. It was not their style of fighting. They liked to fight in the open. General Stark's men were pouring it on, shredding the ranks of the grenadiers. Still they held their ground, fired and continued to close the distance between themselves and the Continentals, impressing Thomas with their courage and discipline.

The grenadiers moved to within fifty yards and stopped. One of their officers gave the commands, "load, make ready, take aim, fire!"

Snap-boom! The British Grenadiers fired in unison. As every order was given, they moved like one soldier. Thomas now understood why these men were so difficult to beat on the open field. Despite the musket fire they were taking from a mostly hidden enemy, they stood their ground, displaying stoic looks of determination. Even though several red clad comrades were shot down, the others continued to load and fire methodically as if they weren't in any danger at all. Thomas heard the British officer order his men to fire at will.

The Continentals were protected, but the accuracy of the British Brown Bess muskets and the discipline of the troops began taking their toll. Thomas heard the screams of men from Stark's command as musket balls struck home. The Continentals began to abandon their cover and move back. The grenadiers, noticing a weakening enemy, continued their advance. The red coat columns stopped once they reached the middle of town and continued to fire at the slowly withdrawing enemy. It occurred to Thomas that they must be waiting for something. He was right.

Despite the incredible noise coming from the roar of the guns, Thomas heard the roll of drums beating from the direction of the forest. He saw another force moving through the edge of the trees. They weren't wearing the red coats of the British Army; they were wearing blue and yellow, and had odd conical caps on top of their heads that reflected the sunlight. The caps were topped with red, and many of the men wore mustaches of various lengths. He had heard of these men before, but had figured they were just a bedtime story that mothers told disobedient children. In front of him was a nightmare come to life. Thomas moaned.

"Hessians!" *Can it get any worse for us?*

It was clear that he wasn't the only one to notice this new threat. He heard the word "Hessians" murmured throughout the town as if it was a declaration that the devil himself had arrived. These German mercenaries had been hired by the British Army to do their dirty work for them. They were rumored to be merciless, and now here they were. The Continentals had been putting up a decent fight, but began to move back even faster. The Hessians reputation for fighting skill had preceded them. Nobody wanted to face them. They were hired killers, and they were very good at their job.

Thomas noticed a pudgy blond figure that had to be the Hessian commander. Even in the midst of battle, he sat on top of his horse, arrogantly daring anyone to strike him. He barked something that Thomas couldn't understand and pointed in the direction of General Stark's men. With a great "Huzzah!" the Hessians joined the British Grenadiers and charged.

General Stark's troops panicked. They were already being pushed back; now many of them were running to the safety of the woods on the other side of the town in full retreat. Stark was frantically trying to get his men to turn and fight, but the sight of the Hessians and the charging grenadiers was too much for them. Thomas fired his last round and moved to join the rest of the men. *We are always running away!* The Hessians and grenadiers were emboldened by the flight of their enemy and now were quickstepping full speed through the town toward where General Stark was trying desperately to rally his men.

Just when it looked like disaster might befall his entire force the long wail of a horn pierced the air. Clear as could be, the note from the horn reached the ears of everyone in town. The Continental soldiers who had been frantically running to the forest stopped.

It was the sweetest thing Thomas had ever heard. He too had quit his flight to the trees to listen. Thomas knew this sound. It was a hunter's horn. He had heard his father use one just like it when gaming with friends and family. It meant that somewhere amidst the oaks and maples there was help. *How much help?* Thomas wondered. He turned back to the town to see what would happen next.

The red coats and Hessians heard the horn as well. They stopped their advance to look nervously in the direction of the sound. It wasn't easy to figure out because the horn's call rebounded off of the forest in endless echoes. Their hesitation was answered by another long wailing note. Thomas couldn't be sure if it was the same horn or another like it. The sound again repeated eerily between the trees and reached everyone within the town.

This time the call from the horn was answered. It started with one and then was joined by what sounded like hundreds of . . . *gobbling turkeys? Am I going crazy?* Thomas shook his head. Maybe the August heat or the overpowering smell of gunpowder had fried his brain. The gobbling didn't stop. It gained in intensity. This could either mean one of two things: Thomas *had* lost it, or they were about to be joined by an entirely different kind of army.

The gobbling continued to rise within the trees, rolling over the Hessians and Grenadiers from all directions. The enemy had no idea what to think of the situation. Battle lines that had been orderly began to disintegrate as men backed away from the hidden danger. Even the hefty Hessian on horseback was caught in a mystified trance. The British officers looked at each other in panic, trying to figure out what was making all of that noise. Thomas's pumped his fist excitedly. He wasn't going crazy at all. He knew without a doubt what (or who) was making that racket. *It's a turkey call! A lot of turkeys!* The local hunters had come to fight.

"Huzzah!" Thomas yelled enthusiastically. There was hope. He began to gobble too.

The gobbling continued for a few seconds longer and then stopped with a third blast from a horn. Before the British Grenadiers and Hessians could react, the snap-boom of rifles sizzled from the trees ringing the town, immediately dropping several officers and soldiers. More rounds followed the first, and all of them brutally savaged the lines of the enemy standing in the middle of town. The British Grenadiers and Hessians were getting punished from every direction. Now it was their turn to panic. As more blasts from the trees slammed into their ranks, the British troops and their Hessian allies moved back.

General Stark was not about to lose this opportunity. He managed to get his bewildered men turned around during the barrage from the trees, drew the officer's saber from his hip, and yelled, "Live Free or Die! Charge!" With a heart pounding cheer, the Continentals recovered and hurled themselves into the retreating enemy, who had no choice but to turn and try to fight off their invigorated adversaries.

The British soldiers and Hessians managed to reform their lines and were starting to turn back Stark's troops in the middle of the town when the turkeys decided to attack. Gobbling was replaced by screams and war calls as hundreds of men in hunters' shirts and frocks of different designs streamed into the town from every direction. They enthusiastically smacked headlong into the enemy lines. The hunters had discarded their rifles and were now wielding knives, tomahawks, and even a few swords. The weight of the numbers that hit the enemy forced them back.

Thomas watched the fierce hand-to-hand battle rage in front of him. The arrival of the hunters tipped the scales of battle in the town. The grenadiers and Hessians no longer looked confident like they had when advancing. They weren't used to being resisted, and it showed. For once, defeat was a possibility. They were fighting desperately to survive. The tan clad hunters continued to swarm in from every direction at once. Thomas was out of ammunition and knew he could do little good with his rifle. It was too light to be any real use in hand-to-hand fighting and didn't have a bayonet. His short hunting knife would be worthless. He was forced to be a spectator. As he watched the brutality on the green, he decided this wasn't such a bad thing.

It wasn't long before he picked out one shape brandishing a long hunter's knife and flowing within the battle. "Uncle Morgan!" Thomas called to him without success. He watched with anxiety as his Uncle threw himself at the enemy's ranks again and again. Finally, he disappeared amongst a mass of men and didn't come back out. *I can't lose you too!*

****

Lieutenant Baum, of the British Army, couldn't believe his eyes. Everything had been going just as planned. His men, along with Von Breymann's Hessians, caught the Continental rebels by surprise in the town. His men suffered more casualties than he would have liked because the cowards were hiding and shooting instead of standing in a military line like gentlemen. Soon, however, the professional expertise of his men began winning the day. They *always* triumphed. Today would not be different? This was why he had ordered his entire command forward, not even having a care that they could be flanked from behind. The rebels were too incompetent for such a move. He was wrong.

As the Lieutenant watched the destruction of his finely tuned military machine, he realized just how wrong he had been, and it was going to cost him very dearly. He remembered the words of the prideful General Burgoyne, his commander, *"This army will not retreat!"* Lieutenant Baum's superior officer was in for a disappointment, and the lieutenant would have to take the blame for this failure. His dreams of promotion lay broken at the hands of men who could barely march in a straight line. Still, he had no choice. They were beaten. He began issuing orders he never thought would be necessary in the entire course of this so-called war. "Sound the retreat," he commanded. *Done in by gobbling hunters!*

****

Thomas tensely watched for his uncle, but could not locate him within the brawling mass. The Grenadiers and Hessians were being overwhelmed. Thomas found himself admiring the way they fought anyway. They were terribly outnumbered, but still resisted with fierce determination. A horn blew and the stout Hessian officer began waving his arms for his force to move back into the woods where Thomas had been hunting what seemed like only minutes earlier. The well-trained mercenaries formed a thin line to hold off the charging Continentals so that the rest of the troops could get away. The Grenadiers followed their example and moved back to the trees. Within minutes the town was clear as the enemy made a strategic retreat back the way they had come.

Some of General Stark's men moved into the woods to pursue, but returned quickly. Thomas was close enough to the general to hear one of his men tell him that the Hessians and Grenadiers were moving back to the north. "Do you wish us to pursue them, General?"

General Stark didn't even hesitate. "I don't think so. Let them carry word back to their commanders that we mean to make a fight. They might be harder on their failure than we could be. Besides, we have business to attend to here."

The surprise victory caught everyone off guard. They were not used to success against the British Army.

Hunters and soldiers were hugging each other and even him. Thomas found it hard to be happy when he saw all of the bodies that remained lying on the field of battle, friend and foe. He was snapped out of his thoughts by a clap on the shoulder. He turned to see his uncle smiling around a puff of smoke rising from the old clay pipe in his mouth. Thomas hugged him enthusiastically making his uncle grunt. Then, realizing he was surrounded by other men, Thomas embarrassingly backed away, cleared his throat and smoothed his hunter's frock. "Hello Uncle Morgan." He said trying to sound calm and proper.

"Well, hello to you too, Thomas."

Daniel Morgan was about the same age as Thomas's father. His rounded face and slightly too large nose was dominated by eyes that saw everything at once. Uncle Morgan wore the rifleman's frock that was similar to what Thomas wore. With a pang of sorrow, Thomas remembered that his father wore one exactly like it. On the back was an embroidered cape that Thomas's mom had sewn for them years ago.

"You would have been the last person I'd have

figured to be out here, Thomas. It is wonderful to see you, but I can't imagine you dragged your father out here, too. Did you finally decide to leave him at home then?"

"So, you haven't seen him then?" asked Thomas despairingly.

"Heavens no! He wouldn't be caught dead with our lot." Morgan chuckled. He then caught Thomas's dejected look. "What has happened?"

Thomas related the past few days' events. Daniel Morgan's eyes misted at hearing about his brother-in-law. "Thomas, that man is too stubborn to know when to die. I'm sure he's trying to find you right now." His father and uncle had an excellent relationship, although they disagreed severely over getting involved in the revolution. Daniel Morgan had tried unsuccessfully to get Thomas's father to go with him when General Balderdash led his ill-fated attack on Canada. There were some harsh words the last time they parted, but Thomas doubted either held a grudge. He also told him about Mary and what had happened to her family. "I can't believe the British Army would tolerate that kind of brutality from the Iroquois. We are up against a very dangerous force."

After some time, General Stark found his way over to where the two of them stood. He saluted Thomas's uncle. "Thank you, Daniel. That was a timely arrival." He pointed to the horn now hanging silently at Morgan's waist.

Colonel Morgan smiled, "Happy to pitch in. Our scouts informed us that the enemy might be moving in this direction. We didn't want to miss all the fun. I didn't expect to see the Hessians though."

"We didn't expect to see any of them." responded Stark. "I don't understand how the British Army always seems to be one step ahead of us. It is very unnerving."

A horrifying thought struck Thomas. "General? If the red coats knew we would be here, I'm sure they figured out the supplies would be here, too. Is it possible that they know the rest of the army is at Fort Edward? With our forces divided, and supplies low at the fort it might make for an excellent opportunity to attack." Thomas saw his uncle and the general frown as if considering the possibility.

"The weather and the road blocks would slow

down an attack by the army," answered General Stark.

Daniel Morgan took a puff of his pipe and nodded, "Yes, you may be right, General, but if the Iroquois are involved, those road blocks wouldn't stop them."

Thomas envisioned a ferocious Mohawk with a scar on his chest attacking the fort. "Mary!" Thomas wailed out loud, "We have to get back!"

General Stark shook his head sympathetically. "I have to escort the supplies to Stillwater, Thomas. That is my number one responsibility. I'm sure General Arnold can take care of things at the fort."

Daniel Morgan's eyebrows rose at the mention of General Arnold. "Where is General Schuyler? I thought he was in charge?"

"He was recalled to Philadelphia. Balderdash has the command, but he left for Stillwater to *organize* our defenses there."

Thomas's uncle made a face like he had bit into a sour apple. "That man is a coward and a fool. The hunters will not come and fight as long as he is in charge." Thomas figured that General Stark agreed but couldn't officially say so. The look on his face was confirmation enough.

"General, if the Iroquois attack the fort, General Arnold may need help. Your force can secure the supplies here. I will ask some of the hunters if they are up for a little more travel. Maybe we can help him. With luck Benedict Arnold moved the army south to Stillwater before trouble began."

"Your hunters are militia, Colonel Morgan, and as militia you may come and go as you please. If going to General Arnold is what you want to do, go ahead. It would be easier for you to move your riflemen back through the woods. Be careful, there is no telling what other forces the British Army may have out there. We have had very little information." General Stark gestured towards the trees and then turned his attention to Thomas. "I imagine you will go with your uncle then?"

"Yes sir, if you don't mind."

"I don't mind at all young man. Thank you for your help. We can always use good men like you."

Thomas never heard the compliment, his thoughts, and heart were already at Fort Edward. *I hope that silly little girl is alright. Please, Mary, be ok!* The possibilities Thomas imagined were not pleasant.

7

Thomas wanted to take off right away, but his uncle stalled him until he could organize the men. Not all of the hunters volunteered to come with them, most wanted to return home to protect their families. Daniel Morgan told them Thomas's tale about the savagery of the Iroquois war party. Thomas couldn't blame the hunters for trying to avoid the same fate for their own kin. He was also sure that several of the men refused to come because they couldn't stand the thought of taking orders from General Balderdash. After watching the man up close, Thomas couldn't fault them for that either.

General Stark gave Daniel Morgan messages to transport to Benedict Arnold, and he promised to make haste with the supplies to Stillwater, about ten miles to the west. It wouldn't be easy in the rain soaked forest. After final good-byes they began the journey back towards Fort Edward.

To their dismay, it began pouring again. The

hunters did not bring anything with them that they couldn't carry, but given the wet and tough terrain, it took a long time just to move a short distance. They also had to be careful that they didn't blunder into the retreating grenadiers and Hessians. The footing was horrible. Thomas was experienced with wet travel, and even he slipped and fell more than once in the mud. He was so worried about Mary he hardly noticed. Thomas found himself constantly looking back at the others, hoping they would hurry. On more than one occasion, his uncle had to caution Thomas to slow down, so he wouldn't break something or stumble into trouble they weren't prepared to face.

    The battle at Bennington had taken much of the day away, and now darkness surrounded the travelers. Thomas insisted that they keep moving despite the dark, but eventually his Uncle Morgan had to stop them for the night. Nobody was excited about sleeping out in the rain, but many of these men were hunters and were accustomed to spending nights like this. Thomas didn't hide his frustration about his uncle's plan to stop. He knew, of course, that arguing with him was very much like arguing with his father . . . useless. Thomas had half a mind to go on by himself, but his uncle reminded him that if he ran into the Iroquois, or even the Hessians, he wouldn't do much good to anybody dead.

Thomas did his best to find shelter from the rain under a pine tree and plopped down on the soaked ground. During part of their journey they had passed close to a grove of apple trees. Thomas plucked one of the apples that he had just picked and grumpily munched on it. When finished, he curled up in the damp needles and closed his eyes. He tried to ignore the rain and mud-soaked stench that emanated from the ground. The exhilaration of the battle had worn him out, but Thomas couldn't sleep. *What if the Iroquois did attack? Mary would be too stubborn to run .That fool girl would stick her nose right in the middle of the battle with nothing more than a spoon. How dare she make me worry about her like this.* It was a restless night. When sleep finally came, Thomas dreamed of Anachout.

Thomas was awakened by his uncle, and within moments they were moving again. Daniel Morgan sensed the urgency Thomas felt and made sure they were up early.

The rain continued, and it was several more frustrating days and miserable nights before they arrived in the vicinity of Fort Edward.

Morgan spread his militia out just in case the enemy was in the area. The hunters approached the fort slowly, watching for any movement. It wasn't long before it became obvious that there wasn't any, none at all. Even this early, people should have been up and going about chores. There wasn't anybody in sight. Thomas could not bear to wait any longer and, despite warnings from his uncle, sprinted for the fort.

There wasn't much left. Smoke and smoldering fires engulfed what was left of the walls and the houses outside of the fort. Supplies were scattered about as if dropped or forgotten. Bodies of the fallen lay strewn everywhere. One ghastly look at them confirmed who was responsible for this destruction. The Iroquois had claimed more victims.

Thomas frantically ran through the remains of the fort looking for Mary, but fortunately she was not among the dead. Then, he saw it, lying in the dirt. His heart sank.

Thomas reached down and picked up Mary's silver plated pistol. *She would have never left this*, he thought as tears welled in his eyes.

"It looks like a majority of them got out safely," said Daniel Morgan looking around grimly.

Thomas wiped his eyes and placed Mary's pistol in his haversack. "I hope you are right," he sniffed. *My father and now Mary.*

His uncle gave him a pat on the shoulder, "Arnold and the others can handle themselves. I'm sure they are on their way to Stillwater right now. We should bury the bodies quickly before moving on," his uncle said solemnly to one of the hunters who joined them. "Who knows when the Iroquois might return?"

Thomas's eyes drifted to a fallen Continental soldier and shuddered. "I don't want to be here when they do."

****

Mary slowly opened her eyes. *Where am I?* The last

thing she remembered was the massive fist of the Mohawk crashing into the side of her head. She wanted to rub the dull ache that still remained, but couldn't. Her hands were bound behind her around a tree. Her legs were also tied, and there was a piece of cloth in her mouth to keep her silent.

Why didn't he just kill me the way he did all of the others? Mary kept thinking about what had happened at Fort Edward. The Iroquois had come in the middle of the night in the rain. Sentries were posted outside of the fort to warn of an attack, but they never had a chance. The Mohawks used the dark to once again cover their movements and were inside the fort before much of an alarm was raised. The entire force at Fort Edward would have been destroyed if it hadn't been for the quick thinking of Benedict Arnold who was able to rally the defenders despite being taken completely by surprise. It was only through his leadership that a majority of the army was able to slip south during the fighting, his leadership and the sacrifice of those who gave their lives so the rest had a chance to get out.

Mary was supposed to be among the first heading south, but she had refused to leave until she saw to it that every wounded soldier in the fort was safely on his way. The Mohawk found her when she was making a final check. She shivered at the memory of coming face-to-face with the same colossal warrior that they had confronted outside of Ticonderoga. She would never forget the satisfied smile on his face when he realized who she was. Mary tried to defend herself with her father's pistol, but Anachout swatted it away as if it was a fly. She thought he would kill her with his tomahawk. Instead he knocked her out with one punch.

She surveyed her surroundings now to try and figure out where he had taken her. Mary could here singing and laughing from somewhere close. It sounded like the Iroquois were celebrating another victory. She could smell their cooking fires and lit pipes. The high-pitched whoops and screams were everywhere. She struggled briefly against her bonds, but it was no use. She wasn't going anywhere.

Two figures emerged from the woods ahead of her. The unmistakable Mohawk who had taken her prisoner was one of them. The other one wasn't an Iroquois at all. He was dressed as a high ranking British officer, a general most likely. Mary could tell by the coat. He was clean-shaven, as all British soldiers were, and very handsome. His white wig was tied behind him in a ponytail. The two men kept pointing toward her. By the way the British General was moving his arms and hands she didn't think he was very happy. They came closer and stopped their conversation to stare at her.

"You take a great risk bringing her, Anachout. If she is spotted by one of the other soldiers or officers, there might be some trouble. I sent you in front of the main army to exterminate these people. You were to take scalps not prisoners. Prisoners cause questions. Questions cause difficulties."

Who could this be that he is giving commands to this fearsome brave? Wondered Mary.

"It is my right as a warrior to take a prisoner if I wish. Her life is now mine. I am trading it for the lives her kind has stolen from my people. I will remind her every day as she prepares my meals and washes my clothes. Do you intend to deprive me of this right, White Chief?"

"No, Anachout, I do not wish to deprive you of what you have earned, but you must use caution. The Great White Chief in England will not be pleased when he learns about attacks on women and children."

"Attacks that you commanded, White Chief!"

"Yes, Anachout, attacks that I commanded."

"Attacks that you will take responsibility for if the time comes!"

"I have already told you such several times my friend and ally. These rebel scum need to be taught a lesson. I want them beaten and I want their will to fight squashed. We will be the ones to bring final victory to the White Chief in England. We will be heroes, legends written about in books. Continue to take scalps of the whites. Soldier, woman or child matters not to me. Their scalps are all worth the same. But be mindful that the other white chiefs in camp to do not share the same zeal and hatred of the enemy as I do. They will not understand that your actions are necessary. This is why the taking of a female prisoner is troublesome to me."

The brave grunted, satisfied with the British General's response, and pointed to Mary. "She will be kept away from the other soldiers," grumbled the warrior irritably. "She will not become a problem. No one will question her presence; *our* deal will remain secret?"

Mary couldn't believe what she was hearing. *The red coats have given permission to the Mohawks to kill women and children. This British General wants them to take their scalps! He will pay for what he has done! I will make them all pay!*

The British General noticed the murderous stare Mary was giving him. He walked up to her and lifted her chin with his hand. She wanted to bite him, but the rag in her mouth prevented it. The General flashed a smile as he peered into Mary's face.

"You may still have to train this one; she has fight left in her yet. How did the rest of the attack go?" he asked the massive warrior as he continued to smile fiendishly at Mary.

"The Iroquois Nation took the fort and colored our knives red with the land stealer's blood. Some escaped, but they will carry news of our deeds. Fear will keep many from fighting again."

The General nodded his head.

"I hope your pockets are deep to pay my warriors for the scalps they have taken."

The red coat's wicked grin sickened Mary. "I have that and plenty more for when this job is complete." The British General moved away from Mary with a final fake smile and headed back into the woods toward his command tent.

The hulking Mohawk gave Mary a menacing look and sat across from her. For the first time she noticed an ugly bruise on the right side of his head that helped compliment the scar on his chest. The Mohawk brought a hand up to the bruise and then ferociously used his other hand to grab Mary by the throat.

"So you are awake," he snarled. "My name is Anachout. In your tongue it means The Wasp. For the rest of your life you will feel my sting. I will make you wish that I had killed you. I will make you suffer for all of the suffering your people caused me." His hands moved from his head to where the scar slanted down his chest. "I will make you pay for the wrongs committed to the Iroquois. It was your kind that murdered my family and stole the land of our ancestors. Every day of your life will be a reminder that you have no honor, that your people have no honor. You are a dog to do my bidding now, and for the rest of the life that I, Anachout, the Earth Mother's Avenging Angel, allow you to have."

With that he got up and left. Mary struggled with the bonds that held her. She knew that Anachout held a hatred and pain that would never be satisfied. She didn't care. It was no excuse for what they had done to *her* family and now she knew who was behind it. Mary was learning how to hate as well.

She wrestled against the ropes that held her, but it only deepened the bruises forming on her wrists and ankles, so she stopped. The sounds of Mohawk celebration continued to drift towards her in the night. She tried not to think of what was going to happen to her in the days to come. All she wanted was justice for her family. She had no intention of being a slave for the savage Mohawk who held her prisoner.

"Be still." A voice whispered from behind her. Her restraints were being loosened by someone she could not see. In moments her hands were free. Mary wanted to whirl around to face her rescuer, but a hand was placed on her legs to keep her still. Whoever it was, kept their back to her as they worked on the ropes around her ankles. It was not an Iroquois. This much she could tell. Mary undid the cloth around her mouth.

"Thank you!" she whispered.

As soon as her legs were freed, her hero turned to look at her with a huge grin. "You are welcome, Mary Chapman; but save your thanks until we make it to safety."

Mary almost giggled with joy. The man in front of her looked just like Thomas . . . only older. "Mr. Bowman! You're alive!"

Elden Bowman quickly placed his hand over her mouth and looked around. "Shhh! For now! If you're not quiet, I won't be alive much longer."

"Oh, Thomas will be so happy to see you; he thinks you are dead."

"Yes, well, let's get out of here before his fears become reality."

Thomas's father helped Mary to her feet and began guiding her away from the camp. At first she moved swiftly alongside him but then stopped. "Come on, Mary, we have to go!"

Mary took a step backward. "Mr. Bowman, thank you for rescuing me. Thomas will probably be with the rest of the army in Stillwater. He will be very happy to see you. I have something I need to do. Tell him . . . tell him to try not to trip over his own feet." With that she ran . . . not in the direction Elden Bowman wanted her to, but in the opposite one, the direction that she had seen the British officer go.

****

Elden just shook his head and watched Mary disappear towards the tents of the British Army. *What does she think she is bloody doing? Women are all crazy, no matter how old they are!* He shrugged his shoulders and followed. Somebody had to try and keep her from getting killed, even if that appeared to be what she wanted. *You'll have to wait just a little longer, Thomas.*

8

Mary stayed clear of the soldiers who were carousing by their tents and fires. They made it easy with their boisterous singing and laughter. The words of "Yankee Doodle" drifted to her from one of the campfires. She had heard the words to that song before. The red coats made it up as an insult to the poorly equipped and untrained army of the colonists. *Men and their egos! They are so sure of victory.*

". . . stuck a feather in his cap and called it macaroni!" The raucous laughter that followed the lyrics spurred Mary forward. *They are so full of themselves! I would love to watch them fall flat on their faces!*

The guards standing post weren't paying much attention either. They didn't have much to worry about. With the Iroquois in the camps around them it was highly unlikely that anyone would attack. Mary was able to move around without a problem.

She followed voices to the spot where she saw a

bunch of officers gathered together. She could see the British General that had been talking to Anachout inside the large tent addressing them. Anachout was there as well. He stood in the background using the other end of his tomahawk as a pipe. His presence alone nearly filled the tent. Mary also saw a woman inside. She crept close enough to see gorgeous dark curls framing a stunning face. Mary had no idea who she was and couldn't believe someone this petite and beautiful would keep the company of men so cruel. The woman sipped from a glass and listened to what was being said. A few of the men in the tent wore long mustaches.

British troops don't wear mustaches. Hessians? They have Hessians with them? I hate them all!

The sides of the marquee tent were drawn up to encourage a cool breeze to flow through where the men were meeting. Mary moved closer to hear the British General speak.

"This army will *not* retreat! Is this perfectly clear?" said the General. By the looks of the faces surrounding him in the command tent, Mary figured they understood the message. "Until Bennington, the King's Army had yet to leave the field of battle to the rebels. It will *never* happen again!" The General said, slapping the flat of his saber on his desk. The men in front flinched.

"General Fraser, do we have enough boats to move on the water yet?"

"No, General," responded one of the men, "We have scoured the area for days. Unless we build our own, there isn't anything useful around here. Most likely we will have to stay on the road until we reach a bigger city where suitable transportation might be available."

"Damn!" the general swore. "One bloody road! We have only one road to use through this god forsaken wilderness. A road that has been intolerable with all of the rain, the mud, and now fallen trees blocking our path."

Mary smiled at the mention of "fallen trees" *Thomas's idea!* She knew he would be thrilled to hear this had the effect on the British army that he hoped it would.

The British General regained his composure, straightened his jacket and continued, "No matter, we will make it work all the same. This is just a minor annoyance.

In a few days we will be moving south towards the town of Stillwater. The enemy is fortifying positions there. What they don't know is that coming from behind them on the Mohawk River is an army lead by General St. Leger. St. Leger is being accompanied by another Iroquois war party. I have sent word to General Howe around Philadelphia to move north. We have the rebels trapped and they have no idea what is coming. I have made sure that they have been fed misinformation. Gentlemen, we can end this war right here within the next few weeks if you have the metal to do it! We must fight as if the safety of *our* homes depends on it. We must fight as if *our* families are in danger. We must fight as if *there is* no tomorrow, because if you fail me now, there *won't be* for you."

"Lieutenant Baum's failure at Bennington cost him his rank and he was sent home in disgrace. Don't let it happen to you. This pitiful band that stands in our way is made up of farmers and woodsmen. There is *no chance* that they can withstand the might of the British Army. With the Iroquois and our friends the Hessians, we have a powerful army that the history books will discuss for generations.

One hard charge by us, and they will be begging for surrender and forgiveness. Are my expectations *clear*?"

The "yes sirs" and salutes he received said that they were. Mary saw the determination in their eyes. The officer wanted them motivated by their hopes of glory and the fears of failure.

"It is time that we take our place amongst the greatest of armies!"

"Here, here!" yelled the other British officers.

"Huzzah!" echoed the Hessians.

Listening to the General's speech, Mary became more and more resolved to what she wanted to do. When he mentioned the fighting at Bennington a pain shot through her. *Thomas was headed to Bennington! He better be safe if he knows what's good for him! Probably shot himself with his own rifle.*

The cheers of the men infuriated Mary even more. With every "Huzzah!" her cheeks burned with anger. The General finished speaking and ordered a toast to be poured. When Mary had left Thomas's father she wasn't completely sure what she intended to do. As she hid listening to the British Army's commander, she knew. Mary summoned all the courage she could, moved from her hiding spot, and marched towards the tent.

"Let us have a toast to a great victory and the end to this pitiful rebellion," proclaimed the general.

"To you, General Burgoyne!" chimed one of his officers.

Mary slipped into the tent before the guards had time to react. "Why don't you also toast to the butchering of innocent *women* and children, you *monsters*!"

As soon as Mary's words escaped her lips the guards grabbed her, but not before she made it to the table where the British General was holding his champagne. For just a moment he was completely stunned, but he regained his composure quickly.

"Who is this rude little girl? What is she doing here?" the General demanded, feigning ignorance.

"You know perfectly well who I am, General Burgoyne. I was taken prisoner by your pet Mohawk. I am someone who actually *survived* the attacks you ordered by the Iroquois around Crown Point. My mother and sisters *weren't* as fortunate! Neither were hundreds of others you had *scalped* by *them* for a bounty!" She pointed at Anachout who appeared ready to leap for her throat right in front of everybody. Mary saw the gorgeous woman in the tent put a hand to her face in horror and heard her gasp. "Do they not call you Gentleman Johnny in England? Seems they may be a bit off on that."

The General just sniffed and laughed at her allegations. "That is ridiculous. My army is as professional as they come. If anyone has proved ignorant to civilized tactics in combat it is the very rebels we now chase." The other officers in the tent smiled and nodded at Mary like she was a child throwing a tantrum.

"You lie!" snarled Mary. "They scalped my family on your orders!"

"Certainly not, young lady! The British Army has always discouraged that sort of behavior, and I will not tolerate it here!" The General turned to one of the officers. "General Fraser you command the forward division. Have you seen any of this *supposed* aggression by our Iroquois allies?" The General's emphasis on the word "supposed" brought more than a few chuckles from the men.

"Heaven's no, sir!" said an outraged General Fraser.

"So now, young lady, there you have it. Maybe it was all just a bad dream. You are confused. Your mother is probably waiting for you with a cup of hot tea somewhere." This again encouraged laughter from the men in the tent.

"Baroness Riedesel, have you written about any such violence in your memoirs?" The General asked of the woman who had now composed herself enough to smile sympathetically at Mary.

"No, General, this army has conducted itself with the utmost dignity and honor. I am sorry for your loss, young lady. I have three daughters that are around your age with me right now. I do what I can to keep them from watching the fighting. War is a terrible thing, and it can do awful things to the mind of someone as young as you. I would never want them to imagine anything so horrible."

"I am not *imagining* anything!" Mary was getting nowhere, and she knew it. She had to think fast.

"Someone please escort this young lady to the

outskirts of camp, and send her on her way north. We don't want her alerting our enemy to the south."

"You are a liar and a scoundrel," Mary huffed, stamping her feet.

She figured there was no chance the General would just let her go. She would start on the road north and most certainly be met by Anachout or someone else where they would take her captive again or worse. The two guards at her side began to lead her away. She saw Anachout begin to move from where he was standing. Mary had an idea.

She ripped away from the guards to point straight at the huge Mohawk. "Will you hide behind his words, mighty Anachout? Are you a wasp who has lost his stinger? Are you afraid to admit what you have done? Will you hide in shame because you have dishonored your people by your cruel deeds. Aren't you proud of the scalps you have taken? Some *Avenging Angel*, the Earth Mother is ashamed of your cowardice. A true warrior wouldn't stand silent while this man protects you like a child?" Mary's voice was rising with every word, her anger and grief finally having an outlet.

"My little sisters had more courage. If you had honor you would *admit* to what you have done. Maybe the settlers killed your family because your family didn't have honor *either*! Is this how the Earth Mother's Avenging Angel shows his bravery? Letting others lie to cover up what you do? You are a disgrace to her, your people, and all of your ancestors!"

Before the British General could order his guards to hurry Mary out of the tent, Anachout stepped in front of the soldiers, and in two quick strides, gripped Mary's face in his hand. Again the Baroness gasped.

Anachout's eyes were like two roaring flames that buckled Mary's knees. "I am no coward! I do not hide! I have honor, as did my family! You are the one with no honor! Your people have no honor! This is why it is my *pleasure* to kill all of them and take their scalps, a *pleasure* to kill the women and children, a *pleasure* to help cleanse the earth of all whites. I didn't need a bounty. Their screams were reward enough. The Earth Mother and my ancestors smile with favor on my actions!"

One of the guards holding Mary jumped to stop

Anachout from striking her. Mary heard shocked comments from some of the officers assembled in the tent. *Now what are you going to do, General?* Mary thought. All eyes turned to the British General for his response.

The Baroness moved first. She lunged over to the Mohawk and then jumped to slap him hard to the cheek. With her other hand she hurled the contents of her glass in his face.

"Savage! To think I allowed you to dine at my table with my family! You *are* an animal!" Anachout just sneered as small rivers of liquid ran down his face. He did not even flinch at the sting of the woman's blow that would have brought tears to the eyes of most.

The British General was trying to look just as outraged as the officers around him. "I offered no such deal! This Mohawk acted on his own and without orders! This will not be tolerated! Guards! Put this man under arrest." He swung his arm in Anachout's direction. "The Iroquois Grand Council will be made aware of your actions. You will stand trial for these war crimes. The British Army *does not* condone that sort of behavior!" As he said this he nodded reassuringly towards the baroness who had prudently moved away.

Anachout turned his thunderous glance to the British General. "So, you deny our deal? I acted on *your* orders!" He roared.

"Preposterous!" said the British General indignantly. "Guards! Take him away!"

Before the men could restrain him, Anachout moved. With lightning speed he buried his tomahawk into the two closest guards and downed a third who tried to use his halberd against the brave. As two more guards closed, Anachout's scalping knife appeared in his other hand, and he quickly dispatched them.

Mary wasn't sure who Anachout wanted to go for next. He glanced at General Fraser and a couple of the officers who were loading pistols. "We are not finished, White Chief! You will feel my sting soon! Our alliance is now dead! You and your army will suffer for your lies!" With that he bolted out of the tent more lithely than Mary thought possible for a man that size.

As order was restored in the tent, the British

General faked a sympathetic look for Mary. "It seems I owe you an apology. I am sorry for what has happened to you and your family."

Yeah right, sure you are, you swine!

"I knew nothing of this bounty or their actions towards women and children. That is why we can't trust the savages. You never know what they are capable of. I am sorry for our earlier misunderstanding. I will see to it that your suffering is compensated when this war if over. You are to stay with us for the remainder of the night, but in the morning we are heading south. You are to go north. I can't have you running to your friends in the south and telling them where we are. Escort this young lady to a tent and make sure nothing happens to her."

Mary wanted to make the General admit that he ordered the attacks by the Iroquois, but knew there was no chance of goading him into the same mistake Anachout made. He seemed like the type of man that made lying an art. She would have to be satisfied with the damage she had done. If Anachout did come after her, the General would definitely be next on the brave's list. Mary did her best to sound appreciative of his offer. "Thank you for your hospitality, General," she forced with as little sarcasm as she could.

"I will accompany the young lady if you don't mind, General," said the Baroness. "These shocking events have exhausted me for the evening anyway." The General looked about to protest and then thought better of it.

"As you wish, Baroness, I will look forward to your company another time." "Indeed, General," she politely responded. Mary and the Baroness followed a guard outside and began walking through the camp.

Mary felt she could trust the beautiful blue-eyed woman. "He isn't what you think he is, my lady," Mary said quietly enough so only the two of them could hear. "I know he made that deal with the Iroquois."

The Baroness again gave her a sympathetic smile. "Most men are not what they seem. Still, maybe you are mistaken about General Burgoyne's role in what happened to your family. I find it hard to believe that he could order such a thing or pay a bounty for scalps. His reputation in England is nearly flawless. If he *did* give that order there was no way he could admit it in front of the others. The King would not be pleased with him, and he knows that. Either way, because of you, I don't think that brute of a Mohawk is going to be dining with the General anytime soon."

"That Burgoyne has you all fooled!" Mary said in frustration.

The Baroness laughed. "It would not be the first time I have been misled by a man, my dear girl."

Their armed escort stopped in front of the tent and gestured for Mary to go inside. The Baroness curtsied and then extended her hand. "I am the Baroness Von Reidesel, wife of Frederick Von Riedesel commander of the Hessian forces here under General Burgoyne."

She was very striking. She wore a stunning necklace that sparkled even in the night and wore a beautiful blue silk gown that matched her eyes. It looked very expensive. She smelled as lovely as she dressed. The Baroness looked completely out of place in this wilderness following an army into battle. Mary looked at her own clothes that now seemed like rags compared to those worn by the Baroness. Mary never used to care how she looked; times had changed.

Marie tried to imitate the curtsy of the Baroness and failed miserably. "I am Mary Chapman from Crown Point.

"Well, Miss Chapman, you are a remarkable young lady. I pray that you keep yourself safe in the days to come. The truth always has a way of finding its way out of darkness and into the light. If the prestigious General Burgoyne is a liar, he will be revealed in time."

Mary couldn't help but like the charming woman who stood before her. "I'm not sure how much time we have. It would be better if you all went home."

The Baroness laughed again. "You and I certainly agree on that! Take care, Miss Chapman. You remind me a lot of myself when I was younger. I'm sure my daughters would love your company. Maybe that can be arranged before you leave."

"That would be nice, Baroness. Thank you for understanding."

The Baroness smiled warmly and gracefully walked away. Mary figured a woman like that had to know plenty about boys, and she had plenty of questions.

****

Mary had just settled down to try and sleep when she saw the guard that was posted outside her tent flap saluting somebody, and then he carefully peeked his head inside. Mary wrapped herself in her blanket to cover the tattered white shift she was wearing.

The guard blushed slightly at his intrusion and her discomfort. "I'm sorry, miss, but this arrived for you from the Baroness." He handed her a bundle of what looked like fine cloth. "She wanted you to have these; she says that they are from her daughters' wardrobes and should fit." The guard didn't wait for Mary to reply and ducked back out of the tent.

Mary unfolded the bundle to see the Baroness's gift. She marveled at not one, but two nice dresses that almost matched the elegance of the one worn by the Baroness. They smelled wonderfully clean with a hint of the perfume Mary noticed earlier. She wondered what Thomas would think if he saw her in them. Admonishing herself for thinking that way, she carefully folded the dresses and placed them on a table. *What a remarkable woman. I wonder if I will ever get the chance to thank her.*

Mary lay awake for some time longer. In the morning she would move north as Burgoyne had commanded. After she was a safe distance away, she would find another route to move south. Mary had to warn the army of the trap that they faced. She needed to tell them General Burgoyne's plan of attack. She saw her guard's silhouette outside. Mary thought about escaping. Burgoyne certainly wanted her dead. Would he try tonight? She figured that wouldn't work because then he would have to explain a dead girl that was under his protection. It didn't mean that he wouldn't try some other time. She was very certain that she hadn't seen the last of Anachout. She doubted very much that the Mohawk had just gone home. Mary was going to have to be very careful when she left.

She looked back to the silhouette . . . the guard wasn't there! Before she had time to panic, someone pushed back the flap of the tent and rushed in. "Mr.

Bowman!"

"Quiet my dear girl!" he hissed. "You do seem to have a nasty habit of needing rescued. Although I must say your accommodations are a little better this time."

Mary gave him a hug. "I am free to go tomorrow. You took a big risk following me."

Elden Bowman just shook his head. "No, it is you that took the chance. That was a very brave thing you did and very stupid. You are too young to risk your life like that." Mary was about to argue when Elden covered her mouth. "No time for discussion. I heard everything. There is no way General Burgoyne will let you live; you know too much, and you may have just single handedly destroyed his alliance with the Iroquois."

"That was the idea." Mary said smiling.

"Well, we aren't going to stick around to see what happens next. Let's go!" Mary jumped up to follow him. "This time don't go running in the other direction. I'm getting to old for this sort of adventuring."

Mary smiled at him. "I have no intention of leaving you this time." Mary grabbed the clothes the Baroness had given her and asked Elden to put them in the knapsack he carried.

"Are these really necessary?" he asked with an amused grin.

Mary shoved the dresses into his arms, "Completely necessary!"

"Women," he sighed. Once Elden tucked the dresses away, the pair snuck out of the tent and headed for the woods.

****

Anachout tightened his grip on his tomahawk shaft as he watched the farmer and the girl sneak out of the tent. The Wasp wanted to spring from his position in the trees and sting the two of them once and for all, but he knew it wouldn't be wise. Any sign of a struggle would bring the red clad soldiers. Now was not the time to deal with any of them, but the wait would not be long. Anachout had a plan. He would teach the treacherous White Chief a lesson he would never forget. He wouldn't mind laying his hands on the pretty little Baroness either. Stroking the blade of his tomahawk, Anachout smiled and nodded as the farmer and the girl disappeared through the trees. *Soon! Soon the Earth Mother will receive several sacrifices!*

9

Mary and Elden Bowman silently made their way to the south end of the British Army's camp, stopping when necessary to avoid being seen. Most of the soldiers were asleep. The light from the numerous campfires and lanterns revealed the large size of the force. Mary had to get back to Thomas and the others to warn them of the mighty red tide that was heading their way.

Normally an army deployed a picket line to watch for a possible approach from any direction, there was none tonight. This army was so confident that they didn't see the need for extra protection. They certainly did not fear an attack. Before long, the two of them were away from the tents and heading south on the River Road.

As they walked, Mary filled Elden in on the events over the last several days. He expressed sorrow at learning the fate of her family. Mr. Chapman had been a good friend and hunting companion of his. "War is a horrible thing. That is why I had hoped to keep us safe from it. Now despite what I did, it has descended on us all the same."

"It is a good thing you kept Thomas around. He helped the army more than once already."

"He got his wits from his mother," said Elden smiling.

"I think he got plenty from you as well, Mr. Bowman, even if he forgets to use them sometimes."

Mary told Elden that General Schuyler had left for Philadelphia and had placed Balderdash in charge. It was not welcome news. "That Balderdash is an arrogant fool! It is poor soldiers like him that make it very easy to stay away from the fighting. I knew him when we fought the French. He is incompetent and only concerned about himself. If he is in charge, the Continental Army has bigger problems than just the red coats. Where is General Arnold?" Mary explained that Benedict Arnold was also around, which helped make Elden feel a little better. "They should have given Arnold command a long time ago. That is the problem when you have politicians making decisions about soldiers!" Elden sighed deeply and apologized. "I'm sorry Mary, I tend to get a little worked up over that sort of thing."

Mary smiled. "You and Thomas are more alike than you may think!"

Mary was exhausted and wanted very badly to find some ground to sleep on, but Elden insisted they keep moving. He cautioned her that there was no telling what might be out and about in the woods. After being attacked at Fort Edward, Mary was in no position to argue. By dawn they were already past the abandoned Fort Edward and well on their way south to Stillwater. She half hoped Thomas would be waiting for her there; he wasn't. Mary shivered at the memory of the surprise attack. "It seems like we are always retreating. When will we stand and fight?"

Elden gave her an understanding look. "Hopefully when it is wise my dear girl, and not anytime before."

They turned a little to the west and began following the mighty Hudson River. They passed another abandoned fort named Miller and then crossed the Hudson where it met the Batten Kill River. Here a dam had been built to help divert more water to the Batten Kill and the farmland to the east. The River Road dipped into the old creek bed left dry by the dam.

As they continued, Mary marveled at the glistening water of the Hudson that sped further south. From it you could access most of the colonies. The road they were following now hugged the river along its west bank. It was the only serviceable road to Stillwater and Albany from the Hudson River Valley. On both sides of the Hudson, the land sloped steadily upwards to form a natural trench. The river and the road cut through the middle. It was possible Thomas had been on this road not too long before. *Unless the fool got himself killed at Bennington. He didn't have a Chapman to watch his back. I should have gone with him. I wonder if he is even worried about me?*

The sun had hit its midway point when Mary finally called for a halt. She was worn out and the hot August weather had finally taken its toll. Elden agreed they were far enough away and plopped himself under a sugar maple to cool off. Mary joined him in the shade, but saw the cool waters of the Hudson beckoning just behind them.

"If you don't mind, I am going to freshen myself up a bit."

Elden had his eyes closed for a nap and just shrugged. Mary pulled out from Elden's knapsack one of the dresses the baroness had given her and headed for the river.

She slipped off her moccasins and discarded the filthy clothes she had been wearing for several days. Despite the heat, the water of the Hudson was cool and refreshing. Mary waded in until she was up to her neck and then allowed herself to float like she had done hundreds of times as a child. The area was so lush and green. She wondered if the rest of the colonies were as beautiful. Mary closed her eyes and tried to pick out the different calls of the sparrows and robins that thrived in the area. She soaked in the fragrance of Nannyberry flowers and Rhododendruns. Suddenly she heard braches snapping and the rustling of leaves along the riverbank.

"Mr. Bowman?" No answer.

She dove underwater and swam towards her clothes on the bank. She resurfaced and heard struggling noises coming from the direction where Elden had been resting.

Mary quickly tossed on one of her new dresses, a

wonderful blue one, and then hurried back to Elden. She saw him struggling with someone. Elden was clearly getting the best of the encounter, and by the time she reached them, he had the other man pinned against the ground.

Mary moved around to look into the face of the man. "Reedy!"

The Private gave Mary a cool look. "Farm girl! I see you managed to stay alive," he grunted from the ground, eyes bulging even more than normal.

Mary gestured for Elden to release the disheveled private. As soon as he relinquished his hold on him, Private Reedy popped up, straightened his hunter's jacket and dusted off his hat as if Elden had ruined it.

"Do you know this man, Mary?" Elden inquired.

Mary nodded, "He is a scout for General Balderdash, although I'm not very sure what he is doing here. I would have figured that his lips would be attached to the General's boots."

Reedy snarled at Mary. "I'm observing the area in order to make a report to the General. That's what scouts do you know." The comment was meant to be sarcastic, but Mary almost got the idea that he was trying to make an excuse.

An excuse for what? she wondered. "Well whatever you are doing, there is no need for you to be skulking in the woods."

Reedy just made a nasty face at her and pushed away from Elden. "If you two commoners don't mind I will be on my way."

Elden grabbed the man from behind and spun him around. "Where exactly were you scouting?" he said as he clutched the scout's hunter's jacket. Mary had always thought of Thomas's father as being easy going, right now he looked ready to brawl.

Private Reedy sniffed defiantly at Elden and tried to break his grip on his coat. "I don't have to answer to you. But if you must know, I just came from the outskirts of the British Army's camp and am returning to make my report."

Elden pulled Reedy close to his face. "I scouted that entire area. I never saw you, and I am *very* good at scouting. The only way you were near that camp is if you were inside it, as a *guest*!"

"I should have known you were a red coat spy!" screamed Mary.

"Bah! That is ridiculous!" scoffed Reedy. He placed a foot on Elden's stomach and shoved in order to break away.

"It seems to me that *you* know too much about the British Army's camp yourselves. Wherever that girl goes, the red coats are close behind. Maybe you are spies!"

Mary looked ready to pop him in the mouth, but Private Reedy was already moving rapidly in front of them. "We will see what General Balderdash thinks of all of this!" he said smiling deviously. Without another word he turned and ran down the road.

"We better get moving, Mary. If my hunch is right that man is going to cause us some trouble."

"Do you think he really is a spy?"

"Quite possible. War brings the worst out of some people." Elden looked down the road where Reedy had fled, "and some are just bad to begin with."

They gathered their things quickly and resumed their journey. Mary knew they were getting close because the woods gave way to clear terrain and several houses. It appeared they were abandoned. The inhabitants likely cleared out when the Continentals came through. The owners hearing stories about Iroquois savagery figured there was safety in numbers. *I hope they are right.* Mary worried to herself.

The pair continued their way down the Hudson River Valley. The land continued to rise in a tangle of bushes and trees on either side of the Hudson. Elden identified the area as Dovecot and Bemis Heights. There was still no sign of the Continental Army. The river road now hugged the majestic waters of the Hudson even tighter. They cleared another rise and were able to look down on the bustling town of Stillwater, New York.

"We made it." declared Elden. Mary wasn't so sure how comforting the idea was.

Stillwater, already a decent sized town for this part of the colonies, was bursting at the seams. The two travelers began to pass more and more people, including several soldiers. It appeared that everyone who lived in the area had made their way to Stillwater. Mary saw little children scurrying in every direction. Women went about their chores along the mud-churned road. There were make-shift tents and shelters scattered everywhere. This was as far as the locals wanted to move. Mary and Elden came to a check-in station right before the road emptied into a variety of town streets.

A soldier in a brown military jacket stopped them before they could enter. "State your business." he commanded.

"I am Elden Bowman, and this is Mary Chapman. We bring news to General Balderdash."

Another soldier whispered to the guard who stopped them. The guard nodded at whatever the soldier said and then motioned for Mary and Elden to follow. Mary scanned the crowd in the town for Thomas but couldn't see him. Five more soldiers moved alongside them. She would have liked to believe it was an escort, but it felt more like an armed guard.

"Something feels very wrong about this." she

whispered to Elden. He must have been thinking the same by the worried knit of his eyebrows. They were brought to a building near the middle of the town that General Balderdash commandeered. They were instructed to enter.

The soldiers took Elden's rifle and hunting knife that he carried at his belt. He didn't struggle, but his look of concern intensified. They came to a doorway and were roughly shoved inside.

Mary immediately recognized General Balderdash sitting behind an ornately decorated cedar desk. At his side was none other than Private Reedy who had the look of a tomcat that had just swallowed a mouse. Someone had been smoking tobacco, because Mary was still able to catch the lingering scent.

"So, girl, it seems we meet again." sneered General Balderdash. "Have you brought the British Army with you again?"

"You know darn well we came to warn you at Fort Ticonderoga, but you were too bullheaded to listen!" Mary said, stomping her left foot.

General Balderdash slammed his fist onto the table,

"You will not speak to me in that way!" He took a minute to calm himself, smoothing his spotless regimental jacket. "It appears to me that every time you come around, an attack is quick to follow. Private Reedy here tells me that he saw the two of you coming from the direction of the British Army's camp."

Mary turned bright red. "I was captured at Fort Edward," she stammered furiously. "He rescued me."

General Balderdash dismissed her comment with a wave of the hand. "I'm *sure* he did girl, I'm *sure* he did." Mary was getting very tired of people not believing her.

Before she could tell Balderdash what she thought of him, Elden interrupted. "Sir, if I may. My name is Elden Bowman, I live near Ticonderoga, and I *did* help this girl escape from imprisonment in the British camp."

Reedy leaned over and said something in Balderdash's ear. The General smiled, "I remember you, Mr. Bowman. Amazing that you were able to walk right into the enemy's camp with thousands of red coats, who knows how many Iroquois, rescue this girl, and just stroll right out? A pretty heroic tale if I do say so. Of course so is

Jack and the Beanstalk."

Mary completely lost her temper. "He is telling the truth, General!" Private Reedy laughed at her sarcastically. "Reedy, you toad! You treacherous toad! *You* are the British spy! I should have guessed it before! You have been helping the red coats the whole time!"

Reedy stopped laughing and took a step towards Mary but was restrained by Balderdash. "That will be quite enough out of you, young lady. The private is a very useful asset. You have been nothing but trouble. I think it is more likely that you and your companion here are the spies. I remember Mr. Bowman fighting with the British Army against the French. Maybe he still maintained his friendship with them. Where has he been this whole time we have been fighting? I think it is much more likely the two of you are spies. I'd stake my reputation as an officer on it."

"Not much to go by then." snapped Mary.

General Balderdash's eyes narrowed. Seething with anger he grabbed her cheeks tightly. "Such a sharp tongue. It may be time to dull it!" He released her and motioned towards the guards in the room.

"But, General, you are all about to fall into a--" Mary pleaded.

"Silence you traitor!" Reedy slipped around Balderdash and smacked her in the face before she could finish. Tears immediately filled Mary's eyes. Elden went to pounce on Reedy, but was restrained by the guards who quickly stepped in.

"Take these two to the stockade, and make sure nobody is allowed near them!" General Balderdash ordered. Reedy smiled triumphantly as the two were lead away.

Mary wanted to cry in frustration. *Where is Thomas?*

****

Towards the west along the Mohawk River, General St. Leger of the British Army was trying to enjoy lunch in his tent. Things had not gone the way he had expected. He was supposed to be the jaws of the trap that the Continentals retreating south would never see. He was now bogged down, more trapped than the trapper.

Burgoyne had temporarily promoted St. Leger to brigadier general before the attack on the colonies had begun. They had been friends and gambling buddies for years. It was St. Leger's job to take a combined force of around one thousand men south along the Mohawk River, wiping away whatever resistance crossed their path. They would eventually turn north where the Mohawk River met the Hudson and catch the rebel army from behind. At first things went brilliantly. The Iroquois he had with him under their leader Joseph Brandt had successfully navigated St. Leger's force down through the Mohawk River Valley at a respectable pace ten miles per day. At one point, St. Leger had become concerned that they may be moving too fast. He had visions of rising much higher than brigadier general. Pleasing his friend, Burgoyne, was one way to insure that happened. All was in order until they reached the small town of Oriskany, New York where Fort Stanwix stood in his way.

The people from the surrounding area had come here for protection from the ravaging hordes of Iroquois.

St. Leger's Iroquois allies were given the same orders as those with General Burgoyne, kill and scalp everyone. General St. Leger didn't totally agree with Burgoyne's idea of waging war on women and children and paying a bounty for their scalps, but he had to admit its effectiveness in scaring away the opposition. Besides, his rise to power in the British Army depended greatly on the recommendations of Burgoyne. A fact he was sure Burgoyne relied on for his cooperation. While they had been friends for years, power was more important than friendship. If Burgoyne's deal with the Iroquois was revealed, St. Leger would not be the one to do it . . . unless he had to. Power put money in the coffers, friendship didn't.

St. Leger now had other problems. Fort Stanwix was proving tougher than expected. When St. Leger's army had first approached the fort he had sent in a demand for surrender that was completely ignored. He then tried to attack the fort, but was beaten back by the rebels inside. They were not going to surrender easily. Instead of attacking again and suffering more casualties, St. Leger decided to lay siege to Fort Stanwix. He knew this would cause delays, but he had been ahead of schedule anyway.

The siege was interrupted by a daring attack by the Continentals from within the fort that almost forced St. Leger to retreat. His army stood their ground with the help of the Iroquois, but with casualties mounting and their enemy stubbornly refusing to yield, St. Leger was unable to move along the Mohawk River as planned. Now he was stuck and behind schedule, a failure that would be intolerable to his pal, General Burgoyne, farther to the east. He did *not* want to be blamed for a failed invasion. St. Leger knew he had to find a way around the fort.

He had received reports that the rebel army had moved their main force back to Stillwater. It was a perfect position for St. Leger to bring his British regulars and Iroquois down the Mohawk River and right behind the rebels if he could just figure out how to get by Fort Stanwix. If he could accomplish this, St. Leger would be dining in Albany soon, and the rebellion would be over.

One of his aides interrupted his lunch of fresh trout and potatoes, "Yes what is it?" he said, irritably slopping down what was left of his wine glass. St. Leger hated having meals interrupted.

"Sir, a curious thing just happened." The brigadier general waved his hand impatiently for the aide to continue. "Well, sir, it's the Iroquois. A few hours ago our forward pickets claimed they saw a large Iroquois brave approach our force from the east. He was followed by quite a few others."

St. Leger dropped his utensil and glared at the aide as if to say, *You ruined my meal for this.*

The man now obviously on edge continued. "Well, as I was saying, sir, this Mohawk asked to speak with Joseph Brandt. They were gone for some time, and when they came back . . . well sir . . . they left."

Brandt was the war chief of the Iroquois force that St. Leger had with him. "What do you mean they left?"

The aide was now ringing his hands with agitation.

"They are gone sir . . . the Iroquois . . . all of them, even Brandt and the Iroquois that were with us. Our scouts haven't seen them since."

St Leger shrugged and poured another glass of wine. "I wouldn't worry too much. I'm sure they are discussing battle plans, or engaging in some other savage ritual. They will return when they are- -"

"Yeeea!" Before St. Leger could finish, the air was filled with hundreds of high-pitched yells. The Iroquois war cry had begun. "Oh for goodness sakes can't I enjoy one peaceful meal?"

The general jumped from his table and stomped out of his tent. The war cries continued, making his hair stand on end. Snap-boom! Musket balls were whizzing through the air, slamming into his red-clad soldiers, dropping them screaming to the ground. St. Leger was right about one thing: The Iroquois *had* come back. The snap-boom of musketry could be heard everywhere.

"What in bloody hell is going on?"

Anachout delivered St. Leger his answer personally.

10

Thomas was doing exactly what he always did when upset or frustrated. He found a nice spot in the woods and went hunting. The place he chose was just south of Stillwater in a beautiful area filled with hemlocks and oaks. Summer was on its way out, bringing in fall. Thomas never lost his appreciation at the explosion of browns and oranges that the plethora of trees displayed. A ladybug fluttered from some nearby lilacs and landed on his arm. "I wish I had your life," Thomas muttered. The ladybug unsympathetically ignored him and flew off. As Thomas shifted around in his hiding spot, he let memories of the last few days replay themselves in his mind. Despite the beauty of his surroundings, these memories weighed him down. *I'm all alone.*

After they had left Fort Edward, his uncle and the hunters accompanied Thomas south to rendezvous with the rest of the army at Stillwater. Uncle Morgan didn't promise to stick around very long once they got there, but he indicated he felt responsible for Thomas until his father returned.

It was not a very pleasant journey. Even though he didn't know for sure that Mary was among those that fell prey to the Iroquois, he had this nagging feeling that she was in danger. He was convinced something was wrong. He was worried about Mary and was mad at himself for it. *Fool girl, making me upset like this. When I see her, if I ever see her, I'm going to let her have a piece of my mind. Then I'm sending her to the safest place I can think of.*

Uncle Morgan had noticed Thomas's dark mood and had tried on several occasions to pull him into conversation with no luck. During their journey he explained to Thomas what he knew of the war. Thomas was shocked to learn how poorly the Continental Army had performed in battle after battle. He was glad he had kept himself out of it. He enjoyed hearing his uncle's account of how General Washington had tricked the Hessians at Trenton. Thomas hoped some day he could at least catch a glimpse of the man who was quickly becoming a legend.

On their way to Stillwater, the hunters passed

another fort called Miller that was also empty. After a few more fast-paced miles, they crossed the roaring Hudson where it met another river named Batten Kill and moved onto the river road. Near the Fish Kill River they came upon the rear guard of the Continental Army.

His Uncle Morgan made quick introductions, and they were hustled to where General Arnold was surveying the army's movement from his horse. Thomas quickly learned that his Uncle Morgan and Benedict Arnold where old friends. He remembered the reunion.

"Colonel Morgan, it warms my heart to see you well. We have missed you."

"As I you, General. The army is lucky to still have you around."

Benedict Arnold nearly winced at the praise. "You may be the only one to think so my friend."

Daniel Morgan smiled warmly. "There are many who feel that way, make no mistake of that."

Thomas was just about to interrupt the two old friends and ask about Mary when Colonel Cilley ran to meet them. He looked like he had seen better days. Dirt and sweat marked his face and his officer's garb was a shambles.

"It is good to see you, Thomas. Colonel Morgan, it is a bit of a surprise to find you and your hunters here. There must be a good story behind it. What happened at Bennington?"

Impatience finally got the best of Thomas. "Where is Mary, Colonel Cilley? I'll fill you in, but I want to see her first."

Thomas's heart immediately dropped when he saw the despondent reaction from the men around him.

"I don't know." responded Colonel Cilley regretfully. The Iroquois attacked us in the middle of the night at Edward. It all happened so fast. The last I saw of her she was hustling the wounded out of the fort. I figured she was with them, but when I caught up to them later she wasn't around. One of the soldiers remembered her heading back into the fort. She hasn't been seen since."

The memory of that conversation still made Thomas's stomach drop to his knees. He threw a pebble in frustration and stirred up a few honeybees that were enjoying a nearby fragrant rose bush.

"She better be okay, or I'm gonna kill her myself!" Thomas promised to the colorful trees around him. He let himself remember the rest of what had happened.

After telling Thomas the bad news, Colonel Cilley had put an arm around him for support. "I am sorry, Thomas. She is such a brave lass with remarkable spirit. There is still hope that she got away." Thomas could only look at Cilley and nod, his insides a jumbled mess.

They are gone, first my father and now her.

This was days earlier, but the pain still hammered at Thomas. He remembered being able to squeak enough words out to tell of their victory at Bennington in the Grants. Colonel Cilley clapped at hearing of the "Turkey Call" rescue by the hunters. Colonel Morgan informed General Arnold of the supplies that were being brought by General Stark from Bennington.

As soon as they arrived at Stillwater, Benedict Arnold had been hustled into the headquarters of General Balderdash. When he came out, he didn't look very happy. "The general is determined to make a fight here. Even if we get the supplies that General Stark is bringing, we need more help to have a chance."

Colonel Cilley just frowned and threw up his hands. "That man makes every wrong decision possible. If we wait for the British Army here, they will run over us like stampeding horses."

"Colonel Cilley, as you know, orders are orders." said General Arnold.

"You should have been given command long before this, Benedict! That Balderdash won't be happy until we are all dead. Those fools in Philadelphia do not appreciate all that you have done for us! We should arm the politicians and make *them* fight!"

Thomas figured that General Arnold would like nothing better than to agree with, but he wouldn't be baited. "We do what we have to, Colonel." Cilley just sniffed and kicked at a rock.

"I may have a solution," said Uncle Morgan. "Somebody needs to get to Philadelphia to let them know a fight is coming here. I doubt they will feel comfortable with General Balderdash as the only obstacle to the British

Army and the Hudson River. Since, regrettably, they refuse to put General Arnold in charge. I might be able to bring back somebody that can give us better hope for victory. My men won't stick around here if Balderdash is in charge, but there is someone else that they would fight for. I have friends in Philadelphia who will listen to reason."

"General Washington?" Thomas asked hopefully.

"I wish. I think he may have his hands full defending Philadelphia. No, I'm thinking of General Schuyler. What do you think, Benedict?"

"General Schuyler is definitely preferable," answered General Arnold, "But what if they decide to send somebody else."

"I know who you are concerned about, Benedict, and I understand your feelings, but even *he* is a better option than Balderdash."

Who is "he," Thomas wondered.

Whoever it was, Benedict Arnold was visibly wrestling with his emotions. Finally, General Arnold nodded his head slowly, as if resigning his own fate to something unthinkable. "I don't see that we have any other choice. Whomever they send let Congress know they will get no protest from me."

Daniel Morgan nodded. "You're a good man, Benedict Arnold. Look after my hunters while I am gone. Thomas, keep safe. I'd hate to have to answer to your father." He saluted the officers and dashed away.

"Godspeed, Daniel. Godspeed." said a grim General Arnold.

Thomas was pulled back to the present by a rustle of branches from behind. It was Colonel Cilley. "I've been looking all over for you, Thomas. I have some important news."

"What news?"

"Now before you go charging off like an enraged bull, listen first." Thomas just nodded in agreement. "They are here! In Stillwater! Both of them!"

Thomas jumped up from where he had been sitting. "Do you mean who I think you mean?"

"Your father and Mary are in Stillwater, together." Despite the incredible news, Colonel Cilley did not look as happy as he should. Thomas noticed right away.

"What's wrong? Are they hurt?"

"Other than some bumps and bruises, they are both fit as you could hope." Thomas waited for the inevitable bad part of the news. Colonel Cilley delivered it with concern framing his face. "They have been put in the stockade."

"The stockade! That is ridiculous. What are they doing there? Did Mary punch General Balderdash?

"No, although I wouldn't put that past her."

Thomas began to move in the direction of the town. Colonel Cilley placed himself in his path. "You need to hear me out, Thomas, please."

Thomas figured the colonel wouldn't let him go see them until he had his say. *I've waited a long time. I can wait just a little longer. At least they are alive!*

"They are going to be put on trial tomorrow as spies for the British Army."

"What!" Thomas choked. "What mule-headed son-of-a-goat would put them on trial for that? That is the most goose brained . . ." Thomas shrieked stringing together a series of curses.

Throughout the tirade, Colonel Cilley waited patiently until Thomas exhausted himself. When he finally wound down to inaudible mutters, the colonel finished what he wanted to tell him.

"I never got a chance to talk to them myself. I saw them from a distance. I heard from one of the soldiers inside that it was Private Reedy who accused them. He arrived in town a few minutes before they did and had Balderdash whipped into a frenzy before those two ever made the gates." Thomas was about to explode into another tirade, but Colonel Cilley cut this one off before it started.

"Something isn't right about Private Thorne Reedy. Every time we get into trouble he is nowhere to be found. General Balderdash relies on his information as a scout, but it constantly lands us in harms way. He is always coming and going and never around when we need him. Look at what has happened so far. You and Mary come to warn us at Fort Ticonderoga, he gives a completely different report, and we get attacked- -just like you said. We send General Stark to Bennington to get supplies, and miraculously the British Army arrives and nearly causes disaster. We sit at Fort Edward almost defenseless, and sure enough the Iroquois surprise us. Private Reedy has been giving us bad information since the beginning. If you ask me, he is the spy. He only accused Mary and your father to throw suspicion off of himself."

Thomas digested this logic for a minute, replaying the events of the last week in his own mind. He hadn't trusted Reedy since the first day he met him. Everything Colonel Cilley said made sense. Was it Private Reedy he had seen in the woods right before the British Army's attack at Bennington?

"Could these be coincidences Colonel?"

"A soldier doesn't believe in coincidences, at least not one that wants to stay alive."

That was enough to convince Thomas. "Then we have to assume you are right and Reedy is a spy. If he is and Mary and my father are found guilty, he may convince General Balderdash to kill them both. We have to set things straight. We just have to!"

Another terrible thought struck Thomas. "Colonel,

what are the orders for the army right now?"

"We have been instructed to prepare for a possible attack by the British Army in Stillwater. However, Private Reedy has assured General Balderdash that most of the red coats are staying in Fort Ticonderoga." As the words left the colonel's mouth he realized the danger they faced.

"If we conclude that Reedy is a spy for the British Army, and we assume that General Balderdash's orders are based on his reports, the red coats aren't staying at Ticonderoga; they are heading straight for us! We have to clear my father and Mary and warn the army that the red coats are going to attack." Thomas bolted toward the town with renewed determination. The rolling countryside became a blur as he sped toward Stillwater. *They are alive!* Ignoring his protesting lungs and aching feet, he entered the town still running.

Colonel Cilley followed close on his heels. He was about to head straight for General Balderdash's headquarters when he heard the colonel scream out from behind him, "Thomas, hold!" The urgency in his voice stopped Thomas before he made it to the guards at the front door. "You can't go in there, Thomas."

"We have to tell him what Private Reedy is; we have to explain to him the danger we face. We have to make him listen" Thomas said excitedly.

The seriousness of the colonel's face stopped Thomas. "General Balderdash won't listen to you. Think it through. Robert Balderdash is well-known for bending his ear only to those with influence. I heard from someone that Private Reedy comes from a powerful family in New York. This may or may not be true, but it doesn't matter because Balderdash is more politician than soldier. He won't do anything to offend Reedy if he can help it. He has already shown that he doesn't take your word seriously. If you go in there, he will be forced to believe either you or Private Reedy. Who do you think he will chose? You will end up standing trial like your father and Mary. We need concrete proof that Reedy is a spy. That would force General Balderdash to listen to us."

"How am I supposed to do that?" Thomas moaned in frustration.

"I'm not sure, but we have to try. There are too

many people here to retreat again. There is nowhere else to go. We have to be prepared if a fight is on its way."

"Where is the stockade? I want to see them."

The colonel shook his head. "That wouldn't be wise either. If Private Reedy notices you, how long do you think it would take him to get you tossed in there with them?"

Thomas knew that Colonel Cilley was right, even if he didn't like it. "Couldn't *you* at least go talk to them?"

The colonel shook his head again sympathetically. "And risk Reedy claiming I am in league with them? Not a good idea either. Besides those soldiers aren't letting anyone near the stockade."

Thomas slumped against the wall of one of the town's buildings. "They are so close," he moaned.

"I know lad."

"There has to be a way to get them out of this. I will not let my father and Mary end up in front of a firing squad. If Reedy stays in town, I'll keep my eye on him. Maybe he will give himself away."

"That is a start. I will nose around town and see what else I can dig up. Hopefully, together we can find enough to change the general's mind."

"We have to colonel. Several lives depend on it."

How did we get into this?

****

Thomas made some inquiries and found out that Private Reedy was being quartered in the same building as General Balderdash. The general had commandeered the nicest house in Stillwater that belonged to one of the town's merchants. Naturally he was asked to stay elsewhere while the General made himself comfortable. Thomas found a spot across from the building where he could keep watch and initiated the same ritual he used when hunting. He sat in silence and waited for an opportunity.

****

Time dragged on, but Thomas somehow found enough patience to attend to his mission. At dusk he was rewarded when he saw a lantern from inside get extinguished, and within moments Private Reedy came out of the front door. He looked so sure of himself. He was even humming! Thomas desperately wanted to go throttle him right on the spot. *That will only put me in the same boat as my father and Mary. It would feel pretty good though,* he thought with a self-satisfying smile. He watched Private Reedy move farther down one of the side streets that housed the local taverns. *Hopefully he is out for the night.*

    Thomas looked cautiously in Private Reedy's direction and moved toward the building. He crept along the front and quickly went through an unlocked door. There was just enough light from outside for Thomas to see inside. The first room he encountered appeared to be General Balderdash's office. He figured if Reedy was a spy, no proof would be found there. Farther down the hall, he inched into a second room. This room was very sharply decorated with ornate furniture and a decent-sized bed with brass posts. An oak desk sat alongside the wall. Thomas checked to see if anything was on the desk, but it was clear. He quickly shuffled through the drawers that were also empty. Thomas sighed with disappointment. The top of the bed was clear, but two bags hung invitingly on the posts at the end of it.

Thomas glanced out the window to make sure nobody was coming and moved to the first linen sack that he identified as Private Reedy's haversack. Thomas's heart raced as he reached inside. He heard the clinking of glass, and his hand closed on a small glass object that he gingerly drew out of the bag. It was a vial that looked to have two separate compartments. The upper one had a clear liquid. The bottom one held some sort of yellowish powder. Thomas replaced the vial in the bag and noticed Private Reedy had more than one of them. Interesting, but not the sort of thing Thomas was looking for. *There has to be more!* Thomas wanted to scream in frustration. He slapped the top back down on the haversack and moved to the second bag.

Reedy's knapsack was closed by two leather straps that Thomas hurriedly unbuckled. It wasn't easy with his hands shaking the way they were. Once he had conquered the straps, he flipped the top open of the bag. Peering inside, he shuffled around the contents that appeared to be some cooking utensils, extra clothes, and a variety of odds and ends that once again were no help to him. Groaning louder than he meant to, he redid the strap buckles and looked around the room one more time. *Nothing!* He gave the knapsack a disgusted kick, making it swing from the post.

The motion of the bag allowed Thomas to notice something on the opposite side of it. *Another compartment!* Again his heart raced when he detected that hidden against the linen material of the bag was another pocket almost completely invisible to the eye. Thomas ran his hand along the edge of the secret pocket and then excitedly reached in. His hand closed around what felt like a folded piece of paper. He trembled as he drew it out.

In the dim light of the room Thomas was able to see that what he held was a piece of paper folded to the middle and sealed with wax. Looking closer, he noticed that the wax held the imprint of some sort of insignia. Usually these were made by pressing a ring or other piece of metal into the wax, letting the receiver of the letter know whom it was from. *Is that a royal seal? Is this from the British Army?* Thomas wondered. His breathing quickened as he began to carefully pry the paper apart from the wax. It would be hard to get it to stick again without more wax to seal it, but at the moment he couldn't care less if Private Reedy found out his letter had been opened. Thomas's heart was now pounding against his chest as he folded back the piece of paper and began reading.

General Howe,

The bearer of this letter is to be extended all of the courtesies due to a loyal agent of the British Army. His words are to be taken as mine.

I hope to meet with you soon.

General John Burgoyne

Thomas whistled. *I've got him!*

Click, click, click Thomas heard the unmistakable sound of a pistol's hammer being cocked back to its fullest.

"I knew you would try something stupid, farm boy. A pity you won't live long enough to share that letter with your friends." Thomas turned and looked into the barrel of a pistol held by a grinning Private Reedy. "It will be easy to convince these buffoons that I killed a spy. They may even give me a medal."

Thomas tried to sound brave, but his voice croaked, "No one will believe you." He knew this was untrue, but he had to buy some time.

"General Balderdash will believe me and he is the only one I need to convince. That man is a fool. He thinks I am a son of a powerful family-a lie, of course. Nothing could be further from the truth. I can't wait to tell him about my meager upbringing after the rebels are forced to surrender. Once they do, I will obtain money and power. You unfortunately are not going to be around to see the end." Keeping the pistol pointed at Thomas's face he reached out with his other hand and snatched the letter away.

"Do you think I would really be foolish enough to leave this just laying around? I knew you would do something to clear the name of that girl and your father is it?" Reedy could see his guess struck home. "I figured that you would snoop around if I left. You have been a pain in the neck that I plan on curing right now. After I shoot you, I will show your letter to Balderdash. He will decide you were a spy, with my help, and then will connect you to your companions in the stockade. Maybe he will let me participate in their execution: I think I would like that. With any luck I will have my letter back and be on my way to deliver my message to General Howe. I am to instruct him to move his army of British Regulars north. Between him and the indestructible force that Burgoyne has just a few miles away this pathetic bunch assembled at Stillwater is about to get caught in a trap. They won't have a chance. Once the British Army is victorious, I will be able to drop this little ruse. You are done causing trouble for General Burgoyne and the British Army." Reedy smiled wickedly. "Good-bye, farm boy!" He sneered. Thomas closed his eyes and awaited the shot that would end his life.

11

The shot never came. "You so much as twitch, you die, swine." Colonel Cilley had moved into the room and held his officer's saber across Reedy's throat from behind. "I followed the insect here. I can't wait to watch you die a traitor's death!"

Despite his predicament, the spy smiled, "Bah! That will never happen."

"What is the meaning of this!" demanded General Balderdash as he too entered the room. Two soldiers followed him bayonets ready.

Reedy swatted away Colonel Cilley's saber. "A spy, General Balderdash, I have caught another spy. I found this farm boy in here rummaging through my things, probably looking for more information to take to his friends in the red coat army. I was able to take this from him before you arrived." He sneered at Colonel Cilley and handed the letter to General Balderdash. Private Reedy kept the pistol pointed directly at Thomas's face. Balderdash quickly read the contents of the letter and shook his head.

"This is a very damaging document young man. What do you have to say for yourself?"

Thomas knew he was in big trouble. The general would never listen to him, but he had to try. "I am not the spy, General Balderdash, Private Reedy is. I found that letter in his knapsack. He has been giving you bad information since the beginning. Think about it, every time he tells you something, the exact opposite happens. I even saw him leading the British Grenadiers and Hessians at Bennington."

Reedy made a disgusted sound. "That is ridiculous! I was nowhere near Bennington, and General Balderdash knows that."

Balderdash gave Thomas a hard look. "You are an associate of the other two we have arrested. I remember you from Fort Ticonderoga just before it was attacked. My men have kept an eye on you. You always disappear in the woods, sometimes for many hours. I wonder where you go all of the time. Now I think you have been reporting to the British Army."

"But, General Balderdash," interrupted Colonel

Cilley.

The general gave him a disapproving look. "You may want to watch what you say, Colonel. We will discuss your aggression towards Private Reedy later. Put that weapon away." The Colonel reluctantly sheathed his saber.

Thomas's heart sank. This was exactly what he didn't want to happen. Benedict Arnold was the next to enter. He took one look at Reedy directing the pistol at Thomas and quickly asked what was happening. General Balderdash filled him in with what had transpired, using most of Reedy's version of the confrontation. He handed General Arnold the letter to read as well.

Arnold's face became a mask of controlled fury. "Put that pistol down now, Private!" he screamed at Reedy. Private Reedy set the pistol on the bed and backed away from General Arnold, close enough to Thomas for him to give the spy a hard shove in the back. The guards immediately stepped between the two of them.

Benedict Arnold addressed General Balderdash, "Sir, young Thomas here has helped our cause on more than one occasion."

Balderdash regarded General Arnold with a raised eyebrow. "Yes, General, it *appears* he has helped, but I think it was all just a ploy to gain our trust. He is just like that girl. Wherever they go, trouble follows. A coincidence? I think not." General Balderdash spoke to Benedict Arnold as if he were explaining things to young child. Thomas couldn't figure out how General Arnold was able to put up with the arrogance. "Yes, sir, but--"

"General Arnold, do I need to converse with you privately about the chain of command? Do I need to remind you who is in charge here?"

Thomas saw Arnold grimace slightly. "No, General Balderdash, that won't be necessary."

"Guards, lock this young troublemaker up with the other two. We will hold trial for all three of them tomorrow. I want this army concentrating on the events ahead." Thomas looked at General Arnold and Colonel Cilley for more help, but it was plain they felt just as defeated. Reedy looked victorious as the guards grabbed Thomas and marched him out the door, herding him forward into the night.

They brought him to a stockade that was a converted cooper's shop. It had been abandoned once it became clear that the British Army was coming. Thomas noticed the tools laying on workbenches that hadn't been used in a few days. The guards lead him to another door, opened it, and tossed him inside. The door was slammed and Thomas heard a key turn the lock. The room stunk of dust and decay. There was very little light, and it took Thomas time for his eyes to adjust. He didn't need them to recognize the voice that welcomed him.

"Not exactly the family reunion I had in mind." Thomas turned to follow the sound. He couldn't see well, but Thomas knew he was confronted by a mirror image of himself . . . except older.

"This isn't exactly how I had planned it either, Father."

Thomas wanted to hug him but felt awkward. As much as he cared for him and was happy to see him alive, he didn't want his father to think of him as an emotional little boy. Thomas didn't realize that his father was fighting his own internal battle. He was just as happy to see Thomas alive, but didn't want to seem emotional in a time where he desired to show strength. He didn't need Thomas to worry about what might happen to them. So they just stood regarding each other with amused grins.

"Are all men so stubborn and stupid?" Mary asked, rescuing the two of them by throwing her arms around both. "Thomas, it's nice to see that you haven't managed to shoot yourself."

Thomas grinned defiantly. "I see that *you* still found a way to get into trouble. I thought the worst when I found your father's pistol at Fort Edward."

"You found it?" She asked.

"Balderdash has it along with the rest of our things." Thomas's eyes adjusted enough to reveal Mary in a beautiful blue dress. *Where did she ever get that?* "You, uh, you look nice, Mary."

Mary crossed her arms and "hmmphed" at him loud enough that Thomas was sure the entire town heard. She shoved a finger into his chest. "Don't you go thinking I wore this for you! At least I have enough sense to get clean when I can! I see that the thought never occurred to you!"

Thomas was about to snap back about having better things to do than taking baths when he heard his father clear his throat. "If you two are quite finished, we need to think about how to get out of this mess."

"We are going to need a miracle," muttered Thomas.

For the next several minutes the three of them relayed all of the events that had happened over the last few days. Thomas was shocked at Mary's exploits in the camp of the British Army, the meeting of the baroness, and her encounter with Anachout. *That brave is like a nightmare that won't go away.* He had to admit that Mary's disruption of the British army's alliance with the Mohawks was very sly.

"That should put a little knot in their plans!" said Thomas enthusiastically. "How did you get away from Anachout, father?"

"I ran, really fast. I wasn't about to tangle with that one by myself. He chased me through the woods for a bit, but he had bigger things in mind. Once I figured I was safe, I doubled back and began tracking the Iroquois. It wasn't long before I found the red coat camp. I stuck around to see how big their army is. I hoped to use that information to help Balderdash, even if he doesn't seem very interested in listening. As I followed them, I came across young Mary here. Your parents would have been proud. You are a remarkable young lady."

Mary threw her arms around Elden and kissed him on the cheek. "My hero, twice!" Thomas felt his cheeks growing warm, watching her show affection towards his father.

"That was a neat trick you pulled on Anachout, Mary." Thomas managed to say. "Now that he has turned on the British Army maybe the rest of the Iroquois will too."

"We can only hope, Thomas." Mary said with a sigh. "You have done quite well yourself."

"Mary told me about some of your quick thinking, Thomas. The mind can be a much better weapon than a rifle," he said, smiling proudly.

Thomas basked in his father's compliment. They were usually hard to come by. He told them about the battle at Bennington and his Uncle Morgan. Mary clapped her hands and Elden laughed. "Leave it to Daniel Morgan to make a dramatic entrance."

Elden focused them to the problem at hand. "Reedy has General Balderdash's mind so twisted he won't listen to reason. Before he realizes what has happened General Burgoyne will have us trapped."

"Oh, I hope I get my hands on that Reedy. I'm going to give him a good thumping," Mary said as she rubbed the still sore spot where Reedy and Anachout had hit her.

"What we need is proof that he is lying."

Thomas looked dejectedly at his father. "I had the proof in my hands. Reedy used it to accuse me instead." Thomas went on to explain to them about the letter.

"That Reedy is a sharp one," admitted his father.

"Yeah, well, sometimes a spider can get caught up in his own web of lies. We need to keep him spinning, sooner or later he will make a mistake."

"That is very true, Mary," answered Elden. "I just hope we get another chance." *So do I,* Thomas thought. The three chatted for a little while longer and then settled on the floor to sleep. The room didn't have beds, but at least they had blankets.

"We better rest," Elden said. "Tomorrow could be a long day."

"Or an extremely short one," said Thomas. His father put a reassuring hand on his shoulder. It helped . . . a little. All three slept fitfully. Thomas dreamed of a firing squad that included Balderdash, Reedy, Burgoyne, and Anachout.

****

The innocent trio were rudely awakened in the morning and brought under guard to Balderdash's office. The general was there as was General Arnold who looked like he hadn't slept very much. Private Reedy was there too, grinning like he had just won first place at a town fair. There were also two other officers in the room that Thomas didn't really know along with armed guards. Colonel Cilley was nowhere in sight.

General Balderdash started the proceedings. "You three have been accused of treason against the Continental Army. I have called Generals Poor and Learned to witness. The two generals glanced at the captives haughtily. Under military law we can try this case right now. I have heard all three of your arguments. Do you have anything new to add." Thomas thought for a minute that General Arnold was going to say something, but he remained quiet.

"This is all a mistake, General Balderdash." Thomas began. "It is Private Reedy that--"

"I said something *new*, *boy*!" Balderdash thundered, cutting him off mid sentence. Thomas fought back harsh words and just stared at the general. His father and Mary remained silent.

How can we get Reedy to make a mistake if we can't talk?

"Well, if there is nothing else to say then by the military authority granted me I--"

"Hold on just a minute, General Balderdash." Everyone in the room turned towards the door. The voice belonged to a man decked out in a spotless blue Continental

Army officer's uniform. More than one medal hung on the left side of his coat. He had gold stars sewn into the fabric on his shoulders. He also wore the blue ribband that Balderdash had crossing his white waistcoat. Thomas's Uncle Morgan and Colonel Cilley trailed behind him. The arrival of the new man had an obvious effect on General Balderdash whose eyes widened with shock that turned quickly to anger. The other two generals began shuffling their feet uneasily. Benedict Arnold's jaw clenched like he was being asked to eat a plate of worms.

"General Gates! What is the meaning of--"

"There will be time for that later, General Balderdash," said General Gates with a wave of his hand. "I am under the impression that these three are being tried for treason. I would like to hear their stories."

General Balderdash was visibly trying to regain control of the situation. "All due respect, General Gates, but as commanding officer I have already heard their stories and was about to make a ruling that is well within my power."

Gates nodded and removed a paper from his jacket

that he handed to Balderdash. "Quite true, General, except as you can see by this letter, the situation has changed. By order of the Continental Congress I am now in command of this army."

Gates gave Balderdash a few moments to read the letter. When General Balderdash finished reading he looked like he had just been punched in the gut. "As the new Commander in Chief, I would like to hear what everyone has to say." Gates declared, staring Balderdash into submission.

All three of the captives were given a chance to explain themselves. Each expressed their belief that Reedy was actually a spy for the British Army. On several occasions, Reedy tried to interrupt, but one quick look from General Gates kept him silent. If nothing else, Thomas loved the fact that the spy looked very unsure of himself.

Once they finished speaking, Reedy was allowed to give his story. "General, wherever those two went, the British Army was looming nearby. They acted like they were helping, but what good did they do for us? Are we really to believe that these two could escape the Iroquois war party on several occasions when it appears no one else has been so fortunate? They seem to know every move the British Army is going to make, but conveniently only warn us when it is too late. I personally saw these two coming from the direction of the British Army's camp a few days ago. Look at the dress that girl is wearing. Silk is far too extravagant for a farm girl from these parts. I'm thinking it was a gift for her loyal services."

I also found a letter from General Burgoyne of the British army in the possession of this boy." Reedy indicated Thomas. "This man with the children hasn't volunteered for the army all of the years that we have fought in the area. The only reason he would do that is if he was a loyalist. These three are in league with General Burgoyne, helping to set a trap for us all to fall into. This boy still disappears into the woods, and nobody knows where he goes. For all we know he can be getting reports back to the enemy. My family is renowned in New York for being patriots. I have always been loyal to our cause."

General Gates stared at Reedy for a few moments, rubbing his chin thoughtfully. "Where exactly in New York is your family was from?" asked Gates.

Now Reedy began to shift uneasily. "Further to the east, sir, near Long Island, we have lived in the area for generations."

General Gates stared long and hard at the spy. "Reedy? Hmm, I too have family in the area. I don't remember hearing of any Reedys in those parts. Interesting."

"Well, my family has always kept to themselves," Reedy said like a mouse about to dart from a cat. He must have realized this and straightened. "Look, General, I have served this army faithfully since the beginning, and I tell you this boy and the others are spies!"

Thomas could tell Reedy was beginning to panic. He certainly hadn't expected General Gates to arrive and spoil his execution party. General Balderdash was now looking at Reedy with a very sick expression on his face.

Reedy continued to yell. "This boy on several occasions has been but a step ahead of the British Army. I personally saw *him* at Bennington running out of the woods leading the attack against our troops."

Private Reedy frantically looked at General Balderdash for support. The room was quiet for several agonizing seconds. Balderdash finally broke the silence. "Private Reedy, how could you have *seen* the boy at Bennington? You said last evening you were nowhere near the area! I have a detailed report from you that said you were scouting at least ten miles away from where the battle occurred!" Mary had been right. The spider had spun too many lies and was now caught in his own web.

The room roared into action. Before the guards could snag him, Thomas watched Reedy pull his hand from inside the haversack at his waist and withdraw one of the amber colored glass vials he had discovered the day before. Reedy quickly slammed the vial to the floor. Boom! The considerable explosion that followed sent the startled crowd scurrying for cover. The room immediately filled with a billowing cloud of black and white smoke. Thomas heard something heavy hit the ground. As everyone fumbled around in the smoke, Thomas moved in the direction of the door. Using the walls to guide him through the confusion, he stepped over the motionless body of a guard, and reached the outside. Reedy was in a dead sprint, already several yards away from the building.

Thomas wanted to chase after him, but knew if he went unarmed he could wind up at the other end of the spy's pistol again. General Balderdash stumbled through the door next coughing and screaming for someone to stop Reedy. It was too late. Thomas saw the spy galloping a horse toward the north gates. The sentries never had a chance to stop him. Thomas knew where Reedy was headed.

"Make sure you say hello to that overgrown rat Burgoyne for me!" Mary screamed at the swiftly disappearing spy.

At least he won't be around to cause anymore trouble . . . I hope, Thomas thought. He had a funny feeling that this wouldn't be the last time he would have to deal with Thorne Reedy.

12

Thomas walked back into the still smoky room and looked at the black burn mark where the vial had struck the wood. Tiny shards of amber glass surrounded it. Thomas wished he had swiped one of the small bottles when he had the chance. *What was in that vial?*

"I once owned an apothecary. I've seen something like this before." said Benedict Arnold, picking up one of the small glass pieces. "The vial holds water and sodium, which if mixed together with force, causes the explosion and smoke. It's not something to fool with if you don't know what you are doing."

The unconscious guard would live, but he had a nice bruise already turning purple on the side of his face. Thomas figured Reedy must have decked him with his pistol on his way out.

General Gates was sitting at the desk that had once belonged to Balderdash. "It seems that I arrived just in time. You three have Colonel Morgan and Colonel Cilley to thank for my timely appearance. In fact, I may not have come at all if Colonel Morgan hadn't informed the Congress in Philadelphia as to what was going on up here." As General Gates spoke, Thomas saw Balderdash slink further and further into a wooden chair he was using to keep himself from collapsing.

"I beg your pardon, General Gates, but General Arnold was the one to send me to hasten you to Stillwater. If it wasn't for him we may have buried three loyal patriots." Colonel Cilley said putting his hand on Thomas's shoulder.

"Quite wise of you." said General Gates nodding towards Benedict Arnold.

"Thank you, General." Arnold answered curtly.

Thomas could read absolutely no expression on the face of the now stoic General Arnold. He was acting like a man who was about to be pushed in a direction he didn't want to go. It was obvious the two generals were uneasy around each other. Thomas made a note to ask his uncle what the story was between them.

"Well, I guess introductions are in order. I am General Horatio Gates of the Continental Army, second in command to General Washington. I have been commissioned by the Continental Congress to take charge of the forces here. I have had the pleasure of meeting most of the military men in this room, but I do not know the rest of you. It appears you have had quite an adventure so far."

Thomas's father spoke up first, "I am Elden Bowman, General. This is my son, Thomas, and our friend Mary Chapman. Thank you for helping to clear up this misunderstanding." Elden looked over at the slouching General Balderdash who looked away.

General Gates waved his hand dismissively. "Colonel Morgan informed the Congress of the army's precarious position here. His words were the final push they needed to send me north. As for these accusations you faced . . . we are fortunate that General Balderdash was able to realize his mistake." He too looked at the slumping Balderdash. "Take heart, General, I have a feeling that Reedy fellow has made a living out of misleading others." Balderdash straightened a little . . . just a little.

"Now that we have that settled I believe you may have information that will be helpful. Mr. Bowman, you said that you scouted the enemy's camp before you rescued Miss Chapman. Where are they?"

"Several miles south of Ticonderoga. They are concentrating their entire force in this direction." Thomas watched Balderdash begin to rub his head in his hands.

"I see," responded General Gates gravely. "Do you care to make a guess at the enemy's strength?"

"From what I can tell we will be facing at least three thousand British regulars, almost the same number of Hessians, about four hundred Iroquois braves, and half that number of loyalists from Canada. The army is well provisioned and can bring over one hundred cannons to battle, in all, about seven thousand fighting men. Although, I'm a little skeptical about the participation of the Iroquois at this point."

"Oh?" questioned General Gates raising his eyebrows.

"The brave, but very foolish Miss Chapman here may have caused a bit of a rift between the Iroquois War Chief and General Burgoyne."

"Did she now? Please explain."

"She forced Burgoyne to publicly denounce the Iroquois for scalping women and children for a bounty. Apparently this went against what the General had promised their brutish leader, Anachout. There was a bit of a scuffle afterwards, and the War Chief left quite angry. I have a feeling that wherever Anachout goes, the rest of the Iroquois will follow."

"If the Iroquois have broken their alliance with the British Army it could slow down General Burgoyne's attack. However, even without them, the red coats have assembled an impressive force for sure," General Gates admitted. "You are a thorough scout. I could use you in the days to come, if you intend on staying."

Elden looked over at Thomas, "We'd have to go through the British Army to get home anyway. As long as we are here, we'll pitch in as best we can."

"Excellent, we are happy to have your services," said General Gates.

To the others in the room it may have not have been a significant comment, but to Thomas it meant that his father had resigned himself to get involved in the fight.

Thomas thought it odd that it wasn't long ago that his father's commitment would have made him leap for joy. Thomas's vision of the glories of war had certainly changed. Elden didn't seem to think it a big deal and went to work on a clay pipe stuffed with molasses scented tobacco. The smell made Thomas very hungry.

Mary spoke up. "General, when I was in the redcoats' camp, I overheard them planning. General Burgoyne's army is marching towards us, but they can only use the River Road because they can't find any boats big enough to carry their men and supplies. However, we face additional catastrophe. There is another group of red coats heading down the Mohawk River. They are to come at us from the south."

"If true this is quite troubling," admitted General Gates shaking his head.

"There is more General, I heard them say General Howe was supposed to march north after landing at the Chesapeake Bay. When all the pieces are in place, we may be trapped and facing more than we think."

"Reedy told me about Howe too, General," added

Thomas.

General Gates rubbed his chin in thought. "How far away is Burgoyne?" He asked.

"It will still take him several days to move his entire army down the road to attack us," answered Elden.

"A neat trap Gentleman Johnny Burgoyne has set for us. If that Reedy fellow hadn't been revealed as a spy we would have been caught unprepared," said General Gates shooting a look at Balderdash who was now doubled over in his chair as if he ate some rotten meat.

"However, I'm not entirely convinced that General Howe will move this way no matter what Burgoyne thinks," continued Gates. "With General Washington and the Continental Congress so close in Philadelphia, it may be too tempting of a target for Howe to pass up. It is surprising to hear that Burgoyne is expecting him to march here. It is a brilliant move and one that would have caught us completely off guard. The attack down the Mohawk River is also a stroke of genius. General Burgoyne has authored a masterful plan. Despite his delays, it is too late for us to move further south at this point. We need to prepare to defend here."

"Colonel Morgan, will the hunters stay and fight?" Daniel Morgan had pulled out his own clay pipe and was furiously puffing away.

"Yes, General, and many more may be summoned from the area now that they know you are in charge, and the Iroquois may no longer be a threat." Daniel Morgan shot a glance at the still slumping Balderdash. "However it will take some time to get them moving."

"And General Stark with the supplies from Bennington?" General Gates inquired.

"Probably still days away, General," answered Colonel Cilley.

"Damn!" swore the General. "We will just have to hope they arrive before the red coats."

"I don't think that is going to happen, General." All heads turned to Benedict Arnold who had been silent until now. "There is no doubt in my mind that Reedy is right now informing General Burgoyne of what has happened, and that we may by aware of his entire operation. He will also tell him of our desperate supply situation. As determined as Burgoyne appears to be, he will not want to waste any time, or have his plans ruined. He will send a force to attack us before his main body arrives."

"So we prepare immediately for attack, and make the best of our situation here." announced General Gates.

"No, General, we attack *them!*" answered Benedict Arnold. "It's a move Burgoyne will never see coming. We send a force north and hit them in the woods. Once we bloody their nose, Burgoyne will be forced to pull back and take his time. This will allow General Stark an opportunity to arrive, and for us to be fully supplied and prepared. It will also give the local hunters and militia time to arrive. When Burgoyne finally approaches with his entire army we may have him outnumbered, and we will be in good defensive position."

General Gates remained silent for several moments and finally shook his head. "I don't want to waste valuable men in what could prove to be a deadly encounter further north. We are outnumbered as it is. I don't want to make the situation worse. My order is to make ready to defend here."

"But, General…" began Benedict Arnold.

"My decision is final, General Arnold," commanded General Gates sternly.

"Can we at least send an expedition along the Mohawk River to observe the progress of this second force of red coats under St. Leger?" asked Arnold who looked like he was chewing on a rock.

The two generals stared each other down for a few uneasy moments and then finally General Gates spoke. "Very well, General Arnold, I am going to have you take a regiment up the Mohawk River to see what kind of progress the red coats are making. I know you like to fight, but keep in mind that you only need to figure out their strength, and if practical, slow them up a bit. I need you back here as soon as possible. We don't want an all out brawl, is this clear?"

"I will keep in mind my orders, General." Benedict Arnold said tersely.

"See that you do. If there is nothing else, you are all excused; I have business with General Balderdash here." Thomas didn't think it possible, but Balderdash slunk further into his chair.

13

Once they all filed out of the command house, Thomas listened as Benedict Arnold approached Daniel Morgan. "Do you think I'm right about what to do, Colonel?"

"Yes, Benedict, as always I believe your instincts to be correct. Slowing the red coats down before they get here is imperative. Without General Stark, supplies, and reinforcements we don't stand a chance. Somebody has to go get in the way of the red coats before they can all get here."

"Good! Do you think you are up to the task?"

Daniel Morgan raised his eyebrows at Benedict Arnold. "Do you intend to disobey a direct order then?"

"No. I will do what General Gates has asked. It is important for us to know what is happening along the Mohawk River. Besides, the type of fighting that will be required in the woods is much more the specialty of your men than mine."

"General Gates doesn't want us to move that way,"

said Morgan skeptically.

"Not quite correct," answered Arnold with a smile. "He doesn't want *me* to move that way. As you know, your militia follows your orders, and you aren't obligated to stay here."

Daniel Morgan chuckled, "You really do love to push things, Benedict. That's probably why I like you so much. I think the boys and I would love to take a bit of a walk up north and see what we can stir up."

"Stirring up a bee hive is never a good idea, Daniel," said Thomas's father continuing to puff on his pipe.

"Can't get to the honey without a few stings," answered Colonel Morgan.

"Exactly, that's why I'm going to go with you."

"Excellent!" exclaimed Benedict Arnold. "I will leave you all to attend to my own mission. Good luck. The fate of the army may rest in your hands."

"We will give General Burgoyne something to think about," boasted Thomas's Uncle.

"I believe it, Daniel. Take care of yourselves," said

Benedict Arnold. He then saluted and marched away.

"I'm coming too!" exclaimed Thomas excitedly after the General left.

"You are most certainly not coming, Thomas. There will be plenty for you to do around here," admonished his father.

Thomas was about to argue back when Mary grabbed his arm and changed the subject. "Can somebody please explain to me what is going on between General Gates and General Arnold? It is quite clear they don't like each other very much. Did General Gates have something to do with Arnold being passed over for command?"

"You could say Gates had a lot to do with it," answered Colonel Cilley. "The problems between those two are a combination of politics, pride, and just a bit of silliness."

"I could tell! They looked ready to challenge each other to a duel."

"Don't think for one minute that they haven't considered that as an option at one time or another." chuckled Colonel Cilley.

"For goodness sakes why? They are fighting for the same cause!"

"Yes, but they differ greatly how to go about it. Benedict Arnold is a risk taker, a fighter. Horatio Gates is cautious, more of a thinking man's soldier. Their styles don't mix very well. They respect each other, but they don't trust each other's judgment. It's no secret that Gates has helped to undermine Arnold's reputation to the Congress, despite his many accomplishments. That is why he keeps getting passed over for command. They have been convinced that if General Arnold is left in charge he will do something rash that will lose us the war."

"We can't do much worse." chimed in Colonel Morgan. "Politics! It will be the undoing of us all."

"There are some, Mary, that want General Washington removed as well. Rumor has it that General Gates is one of them." said Colonel Cilley.

"But General Arnold and General Washington are great leaders, aren't they?" asked a bewildered Thomas.

"The finest, but not everyone thinks so. There is a lot of bad blood between many of our high ranking officers."

"Foolish pride." muttered Thomas's father.

"Indeed." Colonel Cilley said sighing. "So now, despite his own misgivings about Gates, General Arnold knew we would be better of with even him in charge. After you were imprisoned, he sent me to hurry the process along. It was a good thing they weren't very far from Stillwater when I found them."

The possibility of what might have happened had General Gates not intervened made Thomas shiver.

"Despite his own ambitions, Benedict Arnold knew we didn't stand a chance against Burgoyne with Balderdash in charge. That was why Colonel Morgan left days ago to fetch somebody else from Philadelphia, even if that meant bringing Gates. Fortunately the Continental Congress agreed to make the change."

"General Arnold may not have liked it, but rather than bogging Philadelphia down with arguments over leadership he would instead step back for the greater cause . . . victory. With General Gates now in command we might be able to convince more people to fight. He knows how to treat every man equally. Not just the rich and influential like Balderdash. General Gates has his faults, but we are in *much* better hands now, and Benedict Arnold knows that."

"The lesser of the two evils." Daniel Morgan agreed motioning towards the command building.

"Exactly." Colonel Cilley said turning back towards the building. "I would *love* to hear what he is saying to Balderdash right now."

"Me too," said Thomas smiling.

"Well, I might as well see if I can be some use to General Arnold. He may want some company up the Mohawk River. With any luck I can shoot a couple of red coats," said Colonel Cilley smiling.

"With any luck they all decided they rather go home," joked Thomas's father.

"We can only hope," admitted the Colonel. "Good bye, everyone, and may God go with you."

"Let's get on about it then, Elden," said Thomas's Uncle after Colonel Cilley left.

"I'll be with you in a moment," he replied turning to Thomas. "Don't be angry with me, son. I just don't think you are ready yet."

Again Thomas was about to argue, but Mary tugged on his arm and intervened. "I'll keep him busy here. I promise."

"See that you do, Mary Chapman. I'll be back soon."

"Please take care of yourself, father. I already thought I lost you once," pleaded Thomas trying hard not to choke up.

"This isn't my first dance, Thomas. I'll be fine. If things get too serious we will get out of there." Elden clasped Thomas on the arm, nodded, and then left following in the direction of Daniel Morgan.

Left all alone Thomas turned to Mary. "What is the big idea? I don't want to be stuck here getting in everybody's way. I want to go with them!"

"Do you honestly think arguing would have gotten you anywhere? It hasn't exactly worked with your father in the past, has it?"

"So what is your point?"

"I have no intention of sticking around here either.

Once your father and the hunters leave we will follow them. Nobody will even know we are gone."

"That's a good idea, but you are staying put. You can't get yourself mixed up in a battle, you're a girl!"

"First of all, I'm a lady, and I'm just as capable as you are! Besides, either you take me with you, or before you have moved a hundred yards I'll let everyone know what you are doing. I also want my pistol back."

"Are all *ladies* this impossible?"

"The smart ones are. Besides, it's always good to have a Chapman around."

Thomas shrugged and sighed. "What choice do I really have?"

"None!" declared Mary smiling.

"Can you at least change out of that ridiculous dress and put on something less conspicuous?"

"Hmmmph! I thought you liked how I looked in this dress?"

"I do…I mean I….I…"

"Oh, you are so much fun to play with, Thomas!" Mary said laughing at Thomas's obvious discomfort.

Thomas just threw up his hands, "Girls!"

Mary continued to laugh as she headed to her quarters to prepare for their journey.

****

A dispirited General Balderdash left General Gates to carry out his orders. The general wanted him to keep a close eye on General Arnold over the upcoming days. Balderdash may have lost his command, but if he played his cards right he could get it back. The General knew for a fact that Gates had been lobbying Congress for his job. He suspected that it was Benedict Arnold who had sent Colonel Morgan to Congress in order to appeal for his removal. Sure he had made some mistakes, but so had Arnold and Gates. Now he might be able to use their mistrust of each other to his advantage. He had worked too hard and given too much to lose what he had gained. Balderdash wanted to defeat the British Army, but he also wanted to be the one credited with doing so. When Gates arrived he thought the chance was lost. Now there might be possibilities. He just wished he could get his hands on Reedy.

****

Several miles to the northwest along the Mohawk River, Anachout was cleaning his pipe tomahawk and scalping blade in the river. The sight of red streaming from his weapons in the clear water pleased him. His braves had destroyed the British troops without too much effort. Their handiwork would be left for all to see. When someone came to find out where the white chief named St. Leger was, their eyes would meet a display that would turn anyone's veins to ice. Except for Anachout's; he had enough ice running through his body already.

Anachout once again glanced down at the red stained water and smiled wickedly. There was more work to be done. Soon there would be a great battle further to the east. He planned on taking part in it. It didn't take Anachout long to convince his Iroquois brothers to come with him. No longer allied with the red clad whites, he and his braves would fight for their own motivations. They had been lied to far too often and it was time to make the whites pay for their treachery. Plenty of enemies meant plenty of scalps. The Iroquois didn't need a bounty to enjoy taking them. *I'm coming for you, White Chief.*

14

With so much to do around town, Mary was correct. Nobody paid much attention to either her or Thomas. They were able to slip out of Stillwater and follow Thomas's father and uncle without to much bother. General Gates was not pleased about the decision of Daniel Morgan, Thomas's father, and the group of nearly one hundred hunters that left Stillwater, but he couldn't stop them because they were considered local militia and not regular army.

With Mary insisting on coming along, Thomas's plan was to stay a safe distance away and observe the hunters in action. He still brought along his rifle just in case. Plus, the Iroquois were still a threat. Nobody could say for certain where they were.

The hunters traveled north along the same River Road that Thomas had been on days before when he first arrived in Stillwater. Their brown hunter's coats blending in almost perfectly with the trunks of the oaks and maples that populated the forest. They moved swiftly, but cautiously, stopping occasionally to use ropes and axes to drop trees along the road to further hinder the red coats probable route of attack.

"There are so few of them, what can they possibly hope to accomplish against a red coat army that big?" whispered Mary while they were stopped.

"They probably won't be facing the whole army. If General Arnold is correct, Burgoyne will only send a few regiments so that they can move faster."

"Will the hunters still be outnumbered?"

"Most definitely," answered Thomas, "but they will try and equalize things using the forest."

"How?"

"You'll see. I have a feeling I know exactly where my father and uncle plan on waiting for the red coats."

The hunters moved further north for a few more hours and then eventually stopped where the River Road dipped down into a fairly steep ravine and continued for about two hundred yards before rising again to the north.

"I knew it," declared Thomas. "This is the perfect spot to set up an ambush."

Under the direction of Daniel Morgan the hunters felled more trees and then fanned out to either side, scaling the tree and brush strewn slopes to take cover on the crest of the ravine overlooking the road. Some of the hunters even climbed trees to get better angles. They would now be able to shoot down at anybody who traveled the River Road with hardly a chance of being hit themselves. Thomas figured the hunters could hold off a force several times their size in this position. Mary and he remained at the southern edge of the ravine so that they had a perfect view, and could watch under cover as the action unfolded.

"On the north end of this ravine is the Batten Kill dam," Thomas explained pointing to a large wooden structure visible on the opposite side of where they lay hidden. "The dam helps to divert more water towards the farmland to the east. It also allowed the River Road to be built along the old creek bed below us."

"I know. You father and I passed it on our way to Stillwater. I used this road a few times with my…" Mary paused, eyes watering. "…my family on trips to Albany. My father helped build that dam," she said wiping her eyes.

Thomas, unsure of what to say, grabbed a couple of pieces of salted pork and offered them to Mary. "I guess now we wait," he said taking a swig from his canteen. Mary could only nod her head and continue to dab at her eyes.

Everyone remained hidden in their positions for what seemed like an eternity. The only sounds coming from nature around them. Listening intently, Thomas could hear the waters of the Batten Kill River to the north, the sound of the moving water interrupted only by the various calls of the forests' inhabitants.

"Look!" Thomas said more loudly than he intended. Mary's eyes followed where he was pointing. Just reaching the north end of the ravine were several figures in green woolen jackets, and red skull caps. They carried bayonet tipped muskets that they held at the ready as they eyed either side of the ravine.

"Are those ours?" whispered Mary.

"Butler's Rangers. Loyalists. Definitely not ours. Benedict Arnold was right!" Thomas's eyes were drawn to a loan, skinny figure, in a red wool cap. The man in the brown hunter's jacket much like his own was leading the Rangers; he knew immediately who it was. "Reedy!"

"I hope he gets what's coming to him!" growled Mary.

The loyalist army, following Reedy's lead, made their way almost to the middle of where the road had been built along the old river bed and was beginning to clear the trees that the hunters had put in their path.

"Why don't we attack?"

"That's why." said Thomas pointing again. Making their way down the road next was a much larger force of British regulars, their sharp red jackets contrasting with the forest around them.

"There are so many," Mary fearfully declared as the line of red coats continued to appear from the north and snake down the road.

Thomas watched as the last of the enemy force made their way into the old river bed. This included several supply wagons, a few pieces of horse drawn artillery and cannon balls. The red clad soldiers halted their march and rested while Reedy directed the loyalist rangers to finish clearing the trees from their path. Thomas estimated about five hundred men in all. The hunters were badly outnumbered.

Just as the last of the trees were being cleared from the road, a long wail from a hunter's horn sounded, and then was answered by another. Before the British soldiers could even regain their feet, the "snap boom" of rifle shots engulfed them from above.

"Let em have it!" Yelled Thomas.

The River Road quickly turned into a cauldron of confusion as men ran this way and that. Officers on horses were trying to give directions, but most went unheard, or were lost in the din of battle. Red and green clad soldiers were desperately trying to scramble up the banks of the ravine in order to close with their unseen enemy, but it was no use. The hunters had set the perfect trap, and were unmercifully pouring it on. Enemy soldiers were dropping left and right. A normally disciplined, professional, British army was in full panic mode. Thomas lost sight of the hated Private Reedy.

"We're winning! We're winning!" exclaimed Mary.

It was then that the Iroquois war call began. First a few and then what seemed like thousands of voices joined in from both sides of the ravine. Muskets and rifles went silent as both armies awaited the new threat. They didn't have to wait long. Screams and yells from the top of the ravine gave in to the sounds of a few "snap booms" and then the sound of metal on metal as hand to hand combat began. Thomas and Mary couldn't see what was happening to the hunters, but it did not sound good.

The British Army that had just moments ago been caught in a maelstrom of destruction was now left peacefully alone in the eye of the storm. That didn't last. Thomas watched as the hunters were forced from both sides of the ravine down to the River Road by what had to be hundreds of Iroquois warriors who streamed after them. Within moments the road turned into a gruesome three way free for all between the British Army, the hunters, and the Iroquois.

"I can't watch this!" Mary cried covering her eyes.

"Father!" yelled Thomas in vain. If he didn't do something fast. His father, his uncle, and surely the rest of the hunters were doomed. He couldn't let that happen. His eyes were drawn to the artillery pieces that were still near the northern end of the River Road. Thomas had an idea.

"You stay right here, Mary, or the next time I see you I'll thump you good!"

"Thomas!" she called, but it was too late. He had taken off towards the chaos down below.

15

Thomas raced into the battle along the road, hurdling tree trunks, and fallen men where they lay. Whoosh! He ducked, avoiding a nasty chop from an Iroquois tomahawk. He ran on, men fighting, and dying, on either side of him. Crack! Thomas brought his rifle up just in time, deflecting a blow from a red coat's saber. He spun away from this latest threat, continuing his flight towards the south end of the ravine, men's screams mixed with the terrifying war calls of the Iroquois. There was no order to this battle; it was survival of the fittest. He doubted very few would make it out of this ravine alive; hunter, red coat, or Iroquois. Thomas gripped his rifle tighter while he ran, but he wasn't here to fight.

Thomas made it to the middle of the ravine when he thought he heard someone call his name. He turned his head, hopefully searching for his father or his uncle. Wham! He was rocked off his feet, rifle spinning from his grasp, by a mountain of muscle, and terror. The horrible scar running down the middle of his obstacle's blood splattered chest identified him.

"Anachout!"

The Mohawk warrior's eyes shone with a deathly light, and he smiled menacingly. "Time for you to feel the sting of the wasp," Anachout said, raising his red stained tomahawk.

Thomas lay helpless, once again paralyzed with fear as the Mohawk advanced. Anachout never made it to him. Two figures in hunter's gear slammed into the enormous man sending him crashing to the ground in a tangle of arms and legs. The combatants separated long enough for Thomas to get a look at who had come to his rescue.

"Father! Uncle Morgan!"

"If I wasn't busy at the moment, Thomas, I might kill you myself," snarled his father. "You have to learn how to listen."

"This is no place for you, Thomas! We won't be able to hold up much longer," echoed Colonel Morgan.

The two men crouched on either side of Anachout, hunting knives drawn. The Mohawk had enough time to pull out his scalping knife and was warily watching both threats, knife in one hand and tomahawk in the other. "We meet again, farmer," the brave growled as if facing two men at the same time was of no worry to him.

"You two old friends?' asked Colonel Morgan circling the dangerous Mohawk.

"We've been introduced before," answered Elden. "Go back to Stillwater, Thomas, right now!"

"I'm going to have to disobey you this time, father," said Thomas regaining his feet. "Uncle Morgan, get as many of the hunters out of the ravine as you can."

"The thought has already occurred to me, Thomas, however we have a bit of a problem here." To emphasize the point, Anachout slashed viciously at Morgan with his tomahawk.

"I'm going to give them something else to worry about. Be ready!" yelled Thomas once again running towards the south end of the ravine.

"Thomas!" he heard his father calling desperately from behind. He couldn't stop, not now. They would all surely die if he did.

Thomas reached a team of horses hauling an

artillery piece that the red coats had left unattended in the attack. Thomas jumped into the saddle of one of the horses towing an artillery piece. Using the reigns, he spun the horses around so that the weapon pointed to the southeast corner of the ravine, directly at the Batten Kill Dam. He then jumped down, and unhitched the team from the weapon. The animals were more than happy to skitter away once they were free from their burden.

    Thomas dashed to a cart loaded with canon balls of different shapes and sizes. He had no idea what the difference was, so he grabbed one from the stack that was the closest. "These things are heavy!" He grunted as he carried the round iron ball over to the artillery piece. Once there he realized he had a big problem. Thomas had never once fired a cannon, he had no idea what to do next.

****

    "If you have any suggestions, now would be a real good time to share," grunted Elden as he picked himself off the ground wiping blood from the corner of his mouth.

"Don't get killed," replied Colonel Morgan panting with exhaustion.

"Brilliant! Thanks!"

So far the two on one contest was not going well for the two hunters. Not only was Anachout impressively large, he was also quick. The brave wasn't having any problem fending off the two of them while dishing out his own punishment. Both Elden and Daniel Morgan sported several cuts and bruises.

"You can't defeat me," snarled the Mohawk. "I am the Earth Mother's Avenging Angel." Anachout quickly spun chopping at Daniel Morgan with his tomahawk and then swiftly turning to slash at Elden with his scalping knife.

"I'm beginning to believe him," groaned Morgan.

"We can't keep this up much longer!" exclaimed Elden, barely escaping the knife and once again tumbling to the ground. Just then the tide of the battle shifted to where they were, combatants intermingling in between Elden, Daniel Morgan, and Anachout.

"I think I know what your son is up to," said

Morgan whipping sweat, dirt and blood from his face. "Tell as many of the men as you can to be ready when I blow my horn," he said tapping the hunting horn hanging at his waist.

"Ready for what?" asked Elden.

"To run like bloody hell!"

****

Ok think! Thomas implored himself. *How much different can a cannon be from firing a rifle?* Thomas thought of his rifle that still lay somewhere back in the ravine. *What would I do first? Powder!* Thomas walked back over to the supply cart and found a cylindrical cloth bag, giving it a shake he knew it to be a powder bag. He grabbed the bag and brought it over to the cannon and dropped it down the barrel. *Ball!* Thomas picked up the heavy iron ball he had brought over and put it in next. *Ramrod!* Thomas found a long wooden pole with cloth wrapped around one end. He stuck the cloth end into the barrel and pushed down the powder bag and cannon ball.

Now what? If this were his rifle he would simply pull the trigger and allow the flint to create a spark and ignite the powder. Cannons didn't have triggers though.

Thomas noticed a three strand cotton rope wrapped around a pole next to the cannon. A quick sniff of the rope revealed that it had been soaked in something. *This must be what they use.* Thomas reached into his haversack and pulled out his flint he used for starting fires. Holding it close to the rope he clicked the flint together and after a few tries was rewarded with the spark he needed to ignite it. *Primer!* If Thomas was firing his rifle he would prime the firing pan with powder. Sure enough he found a powder horn hanging off the cannon near his waist. Thomas grabbed the horn and found a hole in the top and back of the barrel. He quickly poured some powder down the hole and grabbed the pole with the slow burning rope bringing it near the hole on the top of the cannon. "Come on, girl! Fire!" Thomas brought the burning rope down on the hole…a fizzle, then…silence. "Oh bloody hell! What did I do wrong?" Thomas wanted to cry.

"I think you need this, farm boy." Thomas turned to

see Private Reedy holding his cocked pistol in one hand and what looked like a thin iron spike in the other. "The powder bag won't ignite in the barrel unless you pierce it with this first. I'd love to give you a demonstration, but I think it would be more fun just to shoot you." Reedy tossed down the spike and stepped closer to Thomas. "It brings me great satisfaction to watch you die as a failure along with the rest of your pathetic army. You are done getting in our way."

Snap-Boom.

"Ahhhhhh!" The spy cried dropping his pistol and grabbing his arm. Thomas could see red flowing between his fingers. Behind Reedy stood Mary, smoking silver-plated pistol in hand.

"That's for hitting me, swine!"

Reedy began backing away, continuing to clutch the wound with his opposite hand. "You won't succeed. Any of you! We will not be denied our victory!" he then turned and shuffled away.

"Well we will just see about that, spy!" snapped Mary to his back reloading the pistol. "Go ahead, Thomas!"

Thomas grabbed the spike that Reedy had tossed to the ground and plunged it through the opening on the top of the cannon. He then re-primed the hole with powder from the horn. "Here we go!" he said dropping the lit rope on top of the hole.

BOOM!

The cannon rocked backwards with force, the concussion nearly knocking the two of them from their feet. They watched as the ball just missed the dam, sailing harmlessly over the top.

"Missed! I have to adjust the angle and reload!"

"Do it quickly for god sakes." They could hear horns blaring behind them. "The hunters are retreating; the red coats are going to come after us!"

Thomas found a screw attached to a lever at the closed end of the barrel. By turning the lever he watched the barrel of the cannon go up and down. "Just a few turns down should do it!" Thomas said, finishing his adjustments. He then went back through the process of loading the cannon.

"Hurry, Thomas, Hurry!" Mary cried frantically.

Snap-Boom, she fired her pistol into a group of charging red coats stopping them momentarily.

Zip! Zip! Musket balls were now whizzing past their heads.

Thomas finished and brought the burning rope back down towards the primed hole. "Come on!"

BOOM!

The cannon once again rocked back, this time the ball exploded into the dam at the top of the ravine sending a shower of wood in all directions, and then…nothing.

"Great shot, Thomas!"

"Not good enough. The dam is holding. I need to fire again."

"You can't." Mary grabbed his arm and pointed. The red clad soldiers were now nearly on top of them bayonets at the ready. "I don't have time to reload! We have to get away!"

A loud "CRACK" pulled their attention back to the dam. They both looked at each other and at the same time and exclaimed, "Run!"

An enormous rush of water began pouring through

the dam and down the sides of the ravine. Thomas and Mary reached the opposite side and started scrambling up to get away. Many of the hunters had been given enough warning from Colonel Morgan's horn to do the same. The red coats and Iroquois were not as fortunate. As the ravaging tide of water quickly filled the old river bed, many were caught in its path and swept away.

Thomas was almost to the top when he heard a cry for help. Mary had slipped and was desperately hanging on to a branch to save herself from plunging into the racing waters below. He slid down the side of the ravine to reach her. With one hand holding on he reached down and grabbed Mary's wrist. Hauling with all his might he brought her up to where she could get a better hold on the side of the ravine.

"Now we are even! Sometimes it's good to have a Bowman around too."

"Thank you," said Mary panting. "But we aren't even close to being square."

They finished scaling the side of the ravine and slumped underneath an oak, watching the raging waters continue to froth with a wild, untamed, frenzy below them.

"Good to see you two well," said Colonel Morgan who slumped down next to them pulling out his pipe.

Thomas felt a hand on his shoulder and turned to see the stern expression of his father. "Yes. Very good! However when we get back to Stillwater we will have a little chat about your disobedience. I believe this belongs to you?" Elden tossed Thomas's rifle beside him and sat down pulling out his own pipe.

"I'm sorry, father, I just wanted to…"

"I know you just wanted to, Thomas, but sometimes you need to trust my judgment."

"The boy did save us, Elden," chimed in Daniel Morgan.

"How many did we lose?" asked Thomas.

"About half," answered Morgan.

"It's my fault. I didn't know what else to do."

"Don't be, Thomas, we lost many of the men before the dam burst. We were able to get most of the rest out. Without your actions we would have all perished for sure."

Thomas saw his father nod his head. "You did save

us. I guess I can't be too angry with you."

"Go easy on the boy, Elden. Stubbornness seems to run in your family."

"That's for sure," echoed Mary.

"You shouldn't be here either, young lady," admonished Elden.

"Hmmmph!" she replied. "Men simply can't do everything themselves, and it's always good to have a Chapman around!" The three men just nodded, to tired to argue further.

****

Anachout sat on the opposite side of the ravine shaking with anger as the waters continued to wash away his war party, and his latest chance to sting his enemies. He had colored his knife red, but the emptiness and hatred within him demanded more. He knew that in the coming days he would get plenty more opportunities. The Earth Mother's Avenging Angel was far from finished.

16

When the weary and battered group finally made it back to Stillwater they were immediately ushered into General Gates's command post. Benedict Arnold and Colonel Cilley greeted them warmly as they entered. General Gates sat at his desk, he didn't look pleased. General Balderdash stood behind him, regarding each of them with unabashed contempt.

Gates cleared his throat to get their attention. "It has always been the understanding in this army, Colonel Morgan, that the local militias can come and go to serve as they please. We are always happy to have whatever help they can offer. Our cause is as much theirs as it is ours. However, while you serve under *my command* you *will* follow *my* orders or you will find yourselves court marshaled and locked away in the stockade if not at the end of a hangman's rope." As the General spoke his voice intensified.

"I simply can not have men under my command running about engaging the enemy whenever they bloody damn well feel like it! I expressly said that I *did not* want to send a force to the north and yet you went anyway. This type of insubordinate behavior *will not be tolerated!* Is this clear, Colonel Morgan?"

"But General…" began Mary.

"And *you*, young lady," Gates said turning his attention to her, "Have no business skipping around a battlefield with a weapon. That is not how a proper lady should act! I can not have any more of that," the General yelled pounding his desk.

Mary threw her hands on her hips, "I was not skipping…"

Benedict Arnold placed his hand over her mouth, "If I may, General…"

"You may *not*, General Arnold, I have my suspicions that you are behind the actions of these men. If this happens again, you will be relieved of command!"

The two officers stared each other down for a few uncomfortable moments. Finally, General Gates sighed deeply, composing himself. "I must say, however, that your deeds, though defiant and egregious, may have just given this army the break it needs. General Burgoyne will not miss those men as much as he will regret the availability of the River Road to move his army closer to us. With the destruction of the dam it will take him quite some time to get that all figured out. By then we should be fully prepared to give him a warm welcome. I expect General Stark and the supplies from Bennington to be available when Burgoyne gets here. For that I do thank you, and you in particular, young Thomas. Without your quick thinking I do believe all would have been lost. I am sending word of your deeds to Philadelphia. There may be some sort of commendation in it for you."

"Thank you, General, but I couldn't have done it without Miss Chapman. She gave me the chance I needed." Thomas could almost feel Mary beaming with pride next to him.

"Yes, well, be that as it may, thank you all the same. You would make an excellent soldier in this army, and possibly an officer if you wish to put in some time with us."

"I think I've had quite enough soldiering for a

while, sir." Thomas replied.

"Be prepared for more. General Burgoyne has had a leg kicked out from under him, but I don't foresee a man like him packing up and going home. General Arnold why don't you share with them what you found along the Mohawk River to the West."

"The British Army that was approaching us from the west is no longer a threat," explained General Arnold still clearly upset over the rebuke from General Gates.

"Why not?" asked Colonel Morgan.

"It seems they had a bit of a run in with the Iroquois. There wasn't much of them left…at all," answered Colonel Cilley shuddering.

"So as you can see, General Burgoyne has taken a few heavy blows. That coupled with what transpired at the Batten Kill Dam should set him back, but it won't stop him. Not that man, he would rather die himself than admit failure. He's coming with his mighty tide of red coats, but this time…this time we aren't going away. This time we make a stand."

"It's about bloody time!" exclaimed Colonel Cilley.

Everyone in the room nodded with approval.

"Quite so, now if you can all excuse me, I have other business to attend to. Please heed my words. There will be no more of this vigilante sort of soldiering. Orders are orders, have I made myself perfectly clear? This means you as well, Miss Chapman."

"Yes General!" they all replied together.

When they all walked out of the General's command post they were met with what looked to be the entire Continental Army in Stillwater, regular soldiers and militia. Rows and rows of men stood shoulder to shoulder, silent and unmoving, staring at the small band of heroes.

Finally one voice from the back yelled, "Huzzah!" and was echoed by the rest in unison.

"Huzzah!"

"Huzzah!"

"Huzzah!"

They continued to chant fists thrusting into the air.

"Take that, General Burgoyne!" yelled Mary above the cheers.

"You too, King George!" Thomas said smiling. He

had never felt so proud in his whole life.

In the distance an ominous peel of thunder rolled towards them.

END PART ONE

ACKNOWLEDGMENTS

The completion of this project would not have been possible without the unwavering support of my wife, Theresa, and my parents who always seem to believe in me...no matter what.

I need to recognize my students, and my own children, whose energy and enthusiasm for life revitalizes me each and every day. It is because of them I continue to strive to be the best I can. Sometimes, I feel I learn from them as much as they learn from me.

My friends have also played a huge part in keeping this project alive. They have always been there...and there is a little bit of each of them in the characters brought to life on these pages.

A special "Thank You" to Jaime Highfield who helped provide the fantastic cover art for this book. I'm not sure it becomes a reality without her. Thanks also to fellow author Tony Lastoria who gave me the final boot in the rump I needed to get this project out of the depths of my computer and into the world.

And finally, I would certainly be remiss, if I did not thank the brave men and women who fought and sometimes died in the struggle to bring America its independence...we ALL owe you more than we can possibly pay.

Made in the USA
Charleston, SC
23 September 2014